PRAISE FOR
The Memory Thief

"A beautiful tale of beauty and darkness." —*SLJ*

★ "First in the Thirteen Witches series, this
expertly crafted story thrums with magic, love,
and tense action." —*Booklist*, starred review

"A bighearted adventure." —*Kirkus Reviews*

"Will speak to anyone who's ever found comfort
in a book." —*BCCB*

Thirteen WITCHES

BOOK 1

THE MEMORY THIEF

JODI LYNN ANDERSON

ALADDIN

NEW YORK   LONDON   TORONTO   SYDNEY   NEW DELHI

ALADDIN

An imprint of Simon & Schuster Children's Publishing Division
1230 Avenue of the Americas, New York, New York 10020
First Aladdin paperback edition April 2022
Text copyright © 2021 by Jodi Lynn Anderson
Cover illustration copyright © 2021 by Kirbi Fagan
Also available in an Aladdin hardcover edition.
All rights reserved, including the right of reproduction in whole or in part in any form.
ALADDIN and related logo are registered trademarks of Simon & Schuster, Inc.
For information about special discounts for bulk purchases, please contact
Simon & Schuster Special Sales at 1-866-506-1949 or business@simonandschuster.com.
The Simon & Schuster Speakers Bureau can bring authors to your live event. For more information
or to book an event contact the Simon & Schuster Speakers Bureau at 1-866-248-3049
or visit our website at www.simonspeakers.com.
Cover designed by Heather Palisi and Jessica Handelman
Interior designed by Heather Palisi
The text of this book was set in Adobe Caslon Pro.
Manufactured in the United States of America 0822 OFF
2 4 6 8 10 9 7 5 3
The Library of Congress has cataloged the hardcover edition as follows:
Names: Anderson, Jodi Lynn, author.
Title: The memory thief / by Jodi Lynn Anderson.
Description: First Aladdin hardcover edition. | New York : Aladdin, 2021. |
Series: Thirteen witches | Summary: When sixth-grader Rosie begins to see magic, she learns
that her mother's dwindling memory is tied to an age-old battle between the light of the
moon and the darkness of witches.
Identifiers: LCCN 2020003256 (print) | LCCN 2020003257 (ebook) |
ISBN 9781481480215 (hardcover) | ISBN 9781481480222 (pbk) | ISBN 9781481480239 (ebook)
Subjects: CYAC: Witches—Fiction. | Magic—Fiction. |
Mothers and daughters—Fiction. | Memory—Fiction. |
Good and evil—Fiction.
Classification: LCC PZ7.A53675 Mem 2021 (print) | LCC PZ7.A53675 (ebook) |
DDC [Fic]—dc23
LC record available at https://lccn.loc.gov/2020003256
LC ebook record available at https://lccn.loc.gov/2020003257

For Harry, who has rescued me too
many times to count

PROLOGUE

In a stone courtyard at the edge of the woods, a ghost with glowing red eyes floats back and forth past the windows of Saint Ignatius Hospital, waiting for a baby to be born.

In the decades that he's been haunting this place, the ghost has seen it all: visitors and patients coming and going, the hopeless cases, the lucky people with small complaints. He's kept his glowing eyes on the hospital doors in peacetime and during terrible stretches of war. He's seen more babies born than he could ever count.

So when cries drift out through the far west window of the maternity ward, and then relieved laughter, and another set of cries, the ghost knows exactly what it means: a particularly rare event, a miracle magnified. The other ghosts in the courtyard go about their business as usual, unnoticing, but the ghost with the glowing red eyes floats to the window for a glimpse.

Only, then something else happens that the ghost does not expect. Something that, in all the years he's haunted the stone courtyards of Saint Ignatius, he's never seen.

The night, all at once, becomes still. A silence falls over the woods; the dark sky—already moonless—dims. An owl calls to the stars and then goes quiet. A cat consults with a mosquito, eats it, and then scampers off in fear. Leaves whisper to each other a little lower than before. Sensing an approaching darkness, knowing the signs of the presence of a witch, all the ghosts of Saint Ignatius flee—zipping off through walls and into woods, vanishing in the night. All except one . . . who hides . . . and watches.

Slowly two women emerge from the edge of the trees.

The first looks sad and mournful, with a forgettable face, and hands that reach through the air as if grasping for something that isn't there. Strange, translucent moths flutter behind her, and a faint cloud of dust, as if she's just stepped out of a closet full of antiques. The other is far more frightening—with empty powder-blue eyes, the pupils like pinpricks, smudged all around in dark purple circles. She smiles with a hungry mouth full of sharp teeth. From around her neck dangle pocket watches, too many to count.

While the sad, grasping witch flicks a wrist and drifts in through the slowly opening doors, now obscured in a kind of misty haze, the blue-eyed witch waits. The night waits. The animals wait. The air waits. Nurses, doctors, patients coming and going—none of them notice two witches in their midst. The living remain blind to them, as they always are.

Finally, silently—the sad witch emerges through the doors, this time with something bulging under her cloak.

"Is it done?" the second witch asks, and the meek, empty-looking one nods.

"I've laid my curse. The Oaks woman's memories are mine now," she says, moths fluttering out of her sleeves as she speaks. "She won't remember anything—not us, not our secrets, not the *sight,* not even herself."

The second witch considers for a moment, her mouth crooked in bitterness. She glances at the ghostly moths fluttering through the air, then turns her eyes to the lump under her companion's robes.

"And this?" she asks.

"No one will remember *him*, either." The sad witch waves a hand, and the folds of her cloak part to reveal a baby, hovering in the air just in front of her stomach. She smiles down at him. There is something terribly needy and desperate about the smile.

"Strange. The Oakses are always girls," the blue-eyed witch reflects.

The grasping witch clearly longs for the baby. She appears to be the kind of witch who longs for everything. "Can I keep him?" she asks.

The blue-eyed witch fingers the pocket watches around her neck and looks down at the baby with disgust. Then she waves a hand, and the baby floats across the space between them. He begins to cry as the blue-eyed witch glares at him.

"I want no more of this family. The last of them comes with me."

"What will you do with him?" the grasping witch asks.

The other witch smirks, her eyes as blank and endless as a reptile's, and then she gazes in the direction of the sea, though it is too far off to be seen. "It's a fine night for sinking to the bottom of the sea," she says before waving the child toward her, into the folds of her own cloak, which close around him like curtains.

The two witches look at each other meaningfully, their dark hearts beating a thorny, unsteady rhythm. And then, as quickly as they appeared, the witches drift into the forest from which they came.

And—but for the trees and stones and spiders and crickets and cats—nobody sees. Nobody but one curious haunt with glowing red eyes and a rash around his neck.

Ghosts have endless time to fill with talk: stories and rumors and legends to pass the long nights. But because the ghosts have fled, there will be no whispers of this moment later—no rumors of what's occurred—drifting amongst the spirits of the seventh ward.

No one will whisper that when two witches came to Saint Ignatius Hospital to settle an old score and take the memories *and* the firstborn child of a woman named Annabelle Oaks, Annabelle Oaks saw them coming . . . and had just a flash of a moment to hide an infant away. There will be no one to reveal the fatal mistake of a sad and grasping witch confusing one baby for another (a quiet baby, as it turns out; a baby who knew how to keep to herself) . . . of one innocent baby doomed and another saved. Only one ghost knows of these things, and—for reasons of his own—he will not talk.

For now, the crickets in the grass listen in silence for a few moments longer, but then they go back to their chirping. The forest resumes its usual noises. A moment is swallowed into the past.

And a restless, angry spirit keeps his secrets. For a time.

PART 1

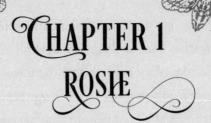

CHAPTER 1
ROSIE

I t's on the night I burn my stories that the danger begins. Or maybe that a *life* begins that's different from the one I knew before.

It starts with me and Germ, the way most things do. I am in the backyard reading Germ a story I wrote.

The story is about a woman asleep in a pile of white feathers. No matter how her daughter tries to wake her, the woman is so deeply asleep, she won't stir. She sleeps for years and years and years.

Then one day the daughter finds a beautiful black iridescent feather buried deep amongst all the white ones. She plucks the black feather, and there is a shudder as all the feathers begin to move. And the girl sees that the pile was never a pile at all but instead that her mother has been sleeping on the back of a giant feathered beast who has been holding her captive and enchanted.

The girl's mother stirs as the beast does. She tumbles off the back of the beast, and together they escape to a remote village at the edge of the earth. Safely hidden, they live happily ever after.

Germ listens in silence and stares out at the ocean as it crashes against the rocks far below my yard. She wraps her coat tighter around herself to ward off the early fall chill. She's got a new look today—thick black eyeliner. It looks weird, and Germ is clearly aware of this, because she keeps swiping at it with her thumb to wipe it away. She's trying to look older but not doing a very good job. I don't know why she tries, because her eyes are pretty as they are.

When I finish and look up at Germ, she frowns out at the water, her brows lowering uncertainly. I can predict something like 1,021 of Germ's moods, and I can tell she's reluctant to say what she's thinking.

"What?" I ask. "You don't like it?"

"I do," she says slowly, stretching and then settling herself again, restless. (Germ never looks natural sitting still.) Her cheeks go a little pinker. "It's just . . ." She looks at me. She scratches the scar on her hand where—at my request—we both cut ourselves when we decided to be blood sisters when we were eight. Her freckles stand out the way they do when she's feeling awkward.

"Don't you think we're getting too old for those kinds of stories?"

I swallow. "What kinds of stories?"

"Well . . . ," Germ says thoughtfully, "the mom waking up." Germ looks sheepish. "The happy ending. Fairy tales."

I look down at the paper, my heart in my throat, because it's so unexpected. Germ has always loved my stories. Stories are how we *met*. And what's the point of writing a story if there isn't a happy ending?

"It's just . . ." Germ flushes, which again makes her freckles stand out. "We're in sixth grade now. Maybe it's time to think about real life more. Like, leave some of the kid stuff behind us."

If anyone else said this to me, I would ignore them, but Germ is my best friend. And she has a point.

Suddenly I find myself studying the two of us—Germ

in her eyeliner and the plaid coat she saved all of last year's Christmas money for; me in my overly large overalls, my too-small T-shirt, my beloved Harry Potter *Lumos* flashlight hanging around my neck like a bad fashion accessory. I've been doing this more and more lately, noticing the ways Germ seems to be getting older while I seem to stay the same.

"Well, I'll revise it," I say lightly, closing my notebook. Germ lets her eyes trail off diplomatically, and shrugs, then smiles.

"It's really clever, though," she says. "I could never come up with that stuff."

I knock her knee with mine companionably. This is the way Germ and I rescue each other—we remind each other what we're good at. Germ, for instance, is the fastest runner in Seaport and can burp extremely loud. I'm very short and quiet, and I'm stubborn and good at making things up.

Now Germ leaps up like a tiger, all athletic energy. "Gotta get home. Mom's making tacos." I feel a twinge of envy for Germ's loud, busy house and for the tacos. "See you at school."

Reaching the driveway, she hops onto her bike and pedals away at top speed. I watch, sad to see her go, and thinking and thinking about what she said, and the possibility of a choice to make.

Inside, the house is dim, and dust scuttles through the light from the windows as I disturb the still air. I walk into the kitchen and tuck my story away into a crevice between the fridge and the counter, frowning. Then I make dinner for me and my mom: two peanut butter and banana sandwiches, some steamed peas because you have to eat vegetables, Twinkies for dessert. I use a chair to climb up to the top shelf over the counter and dig out some chocolate sauce to drizzle onto the Twinkies, scarf my meal down—dessert first—and then put everything else on a tray and carry it up two flights of stairs.

In the slanted attic room at the end of the third-floor hall, my mom sits at her computer, typing notes from a thick reference booklet, her long black hair tucked behind her ears. Her desk is littered with sticky note reminders: *Work. Eat. Take your vitamins.* On her hand she has scribbled in pen simply the word "Rosie."

"Dinner," I say, laying the tray down on the side of her desk. She types for a few more minutes before noticing I'm there. For her job, she does something mind-crushingly boring called data entry. It's mostly typing things from books onto a computer and sending them to her boss, who lives in New York. There is a sticky note on the corner of her computer where she's written down the hours she's supposed to be typing and the contact information of her boss; she never stops early or late.

Against one wall, a small TV stays on while she works, always on the news. Right now there's a story about endangered polar bears that I know will break my heart, so I turn the TV off; Mom doesn't seem to notice. She does that strange thing where she looks at me as if adjusting to the *idea* of me.

Then she turns her eyes to the window in dreamy silence. "He's out there swimming, waiting for me," she says.

I follow her eyes to the ocean. It's the same old thing.

"Who, Mom?" But I don't wait for an answer because there never *is* one. I used to think, when I was little, she was talking about my dad, a fisherman, drowned at sea before I was born. That was before I realized that people who were gone did not swim back.

I fluff up the bed where she sleeps to make it look cozy. She sleeps in the attic because this is the best room for looking at the ocean, but her real room is downstairs. So I've decorated this one for her, lining the shelf with photos of my dad that I found under her bed, one of my mom and dad together, one of me at school, a certificate of archery (from her closet) from a summer camp I guess she used to go to.

I don't have my mom's artistic skills, but I've also painted lots of things on the walls for her. There's something I've labeled *Big Things about Rosie*, which I've illustrated with colored markers. It stretches across years, and it's where I write the things I think are big and important: the date when I lost my first tooth, the date of a trip we took to Adventure Land with my class, the time I won the story contest at the local library, the day I won the spelling bee. I've decorated it with flowers and exclamation points so that it will get her attention. I've also painted a growth chart keeping track of my height (which goes up only very slowly—I'm the shortest person in my class). I've also drawn a family tree on the wall, though it's all just blanks except for me and my mom and dad. I don't know about the rest of my family. I guess we don't really have one.

Still, as strange as it may sound, none of it means anything to her—not *Big Things about Rosie*, not the family tree. It's as if none of it's there. Then again, most of the time it's as if I'm not here either.

"Tell me about the day I was born," I used to say to her, before I knew better.

I knew the *when* and *where* of my birth, but I wanted to know what it had *felt* like to see me for the first time. I wanted to hear my mom say that my arrival was like being handed a pot of gold and a deed to the most beautiful island in Hawaii (which is what Germ's mom says about her).

But eventually I gave up. Because she would only ever look at me for a long time and then say something like, "Honestly, how could I remember something like that?" Flat, exasperated, as if I'd asked her who had won the 1976 World Series.

My mom doesn't give hugs. She's never excited to see me after school or sad to see me leave for the bus. She doesn't ask me where I've been, help me shop, tell me when to go to bed. I've never in my life heard her laugh. She has a degree in art history, but she doesn't ever talk about her professors or what she learned. She never says how she fell in love with my dad or if she loved him at all.

Sometimes when she's talking to me, it's as if my name is on the tip of her tongue for a while before she can retrieve it. Before meetings with my teachers or my pediatrician, she asks me how I'm doing in school and how I'm feeling, as if to catch up before a test. It's all she can do to keep track of the *facts* of me.

I've known for a long time that my mom doesn't look at me the way most moms look at their kids—like a piece of light they don't want to look away from. She barely looks at me at all.

Still, I love her more than anyone else on earth, and I guess it's because she's the only mom I have. My paintings on her wall are one of my many ways of trying to love her into loving me back. And I guess my stories are my way of pretending I can change things: a pretend spell and a pretend beast and a pretend escape to somewhere safe together. And I guess Germ is right that they're never going to work.

And the thing that bothers me is, I've been thinking that too.

I head out into the hall. I flick my *Lumos* flashlight on because one of the chandelier bulbs has burned out, and go down the creaky old stairs to the basement. I throw a load of laundry in, then run up the stairs two at a time because the basement gives me the willies.

On my way through the kitchen, I pick up my story from where it's wedged by the counter.

I have a plan.

And, though I don't mean it to, it's my plan that makes it all begin.

CHAPTER 2

My bedroom is something special, decorated for me by a mom I feel like I've never met. Long ago—before I was born—she painted it in bright beautiful colors, creating rainbows and guardian angels on the ceiling. There's a window around which she painted the words "Look at how a single candle can both defy and define the darkness," which—I found out later—is a quote from Anne Frank's diary. I love the person who painted that on my wall. I dream of that person, but I certainly don't know her.

I've added lots of my own touches over the years. For one, I've filled the room with all the books I've stolen from my mom's room: fiction, histories, biographies, art books, piled on shelves, tucked willy-nilly wherever they aren't supposed to fit, perched on my nightstand. (Other things I've stolen from her include a silver whistle engraved with a shell, a pair of silk slippers, and a matchbox from a restaurant she must have gone to once.) There is a second bed in the room, and a second set of blankets and pillows that my mom has stored in the closet, as if she's always expecting company. I've made the bed a fort for all my old stuffed animals. There's a loud, ticking old clock on the wall.

I've put lots of my own sticky notes on the wall around my bed. *Sleep tight. Don't let the bedbugs bite*. And *Sweet dreams, sweetie*. On the mirror: *You look taller today, sweetie*. And *Those crooked front teeth make you look distinctive, sweetie*. I try to encourage myself with things a normal mom or dad would say, because if I let myself feel sad about not having a normal mom or dad, I'd fall into a black hole and never climb out.

Now I sit on my bed and pull onto my lap the story I was reading to Germ.

I open my closet and take out the pile of others; there

must be a hundred or more. My heart gives a lurch. These stories have always felt like they fill in a half of me that's missing. (I don't know whether it's missing because of my mom, or my dad, or something else, just that it is.) They've always been my way of spinning my feelings into something comforting, like spinning grass into gold. I also retrieve, from my dresser, my lucky pen and my blank notebooks.

I shuffle them all together. Then I carry them down to the metal garbage can that stands outside the kitchen, off the patio, and dump them in. I know how to handle fires just like I know how to fix the refrigerator and reset the furnace and order everything I need on the computer with a credit card—after years of having to do things Mom doesn't.

I get the garden hose unraveled and ready, to be safe. Then I take a match and drop it into the can, and watch the papers begin to burn. All those words I've spent so much time unfolding from my brain—tales of injured dogs that find their way home, elves who give the breathless new sets of lungs, stories about rescues against all odds and lights in the darkness—flame up into ash before my eyes and float away on the ocean breeze.

The firelight flicker illuminates the trees and burns like a beacon in the dark yard. I imagine it must look, from the water, like a miniature lighthouse, the lonely peninsula of Seaport tacked to the eastern edge of Maine like a lonely outpost. Above, the sky lies, cloudy and heavy, over the crescent moon.

I think again about how stories are how Germ and I *met*. On the first day of kindergarten, Germ laid herself at the foot of our classroom door, screaming for her mom. All the other kids steered clear of her—I guess because of the banshee-like wailing. I knew what it was like to miss someone, even though for me it was someone right nearby. So I sat beside the wild-eyed, wild-haired stranger and awkwardly patted her back and told her a story I made up on the spot about a bat who ate ugly old mosquitoes and burped out stars instead. By the end of the story, Germ had stopped crying and I'd won a friend for life.

Now I snap back to attention as the fire sputters out. I close the lid and go inside to get ready for bed.

I ache over what I've done. But Germ is right: my stories are fairy tales I don't really believe in anymore—that anyone can just save the day. I'm too old, I've realized, to hope for things like this.

And despite the ache, I swell a little with pride. Because I think I've figured out the three main things about life:

1. If the person you love most in the world does not love you back, you can't keep hoping they will.
2. If you are not loved (and if nobody cares about polar bears on the news), there is no magic in the world to speak of.
3. If there's no magic in the world to speak of, there's no point to writing stories.

I am done imagining things differently than they are. I feel a distinct tingle behind my eyes and ears and in my heart—as if I have really changed—and I wonder if the tingle is a growing-up thing, and I hope it is.

Outside, the crescent moon glimmers for a moment through the clouds, then is swallowed up by them.

I get into bed and drift off to sleep.

I have changed my life forever. I just don't know it yet.

I wake sometime deep in the night to the sound of someone talking. For a few moments I'm half in and half out of a dream, trying to make sense of what I'm hearing. Then my eyes flutter open and fear sets in.

There is a man whispering outside my door—his voice low and rumbly like sand being shaken in a glass jar.

"The nerve of her. I hate her. Hate her. It's my place. MY PLACE!"

I lie still. The moon peeks out behind a cloud for a moment through the window, then disappears. I stay as stiff as a board, but my heart thuds at my ribs like hooves.

The voice moves off, as if whoever owns it is heading down the hall toward the stairs, though I hear no footsteps. And then, silence.

I wait and wait. Several minutes go by. I start to think maybe I've been dreaming, but my skin crawls. I wish I could get into bed with my mom, tell her I heard something strange. But those wishes have never worked out. I am the protector of this house; no one else is going to do it.

After several long minutes I force myself to silently slide out from under my covers, grabbing my *Lumos* flashlight from my nightstand as I go. I tiptoe to the door, pull it open silently, and peer out into the hall.

There's no one there, but—with a jolt—I hear the voice, still there, though moving away from me and down the stairs.

I step out onto the threshold and peer in both directions as all goes silent again. I tiptoe down the hall and then descend the stairs, my heart thudding.

At the landing I step into the parlor and come to a stop. Because there, hovering in front of the door that leads to the basement, someone is watching me.

He is shimmery and glowing bright blue, frowning at me, his eyebrows low. He floats at least a foot off the ground.

He stares at me for a long moment, as if in surprise. Then he turns and floats through the door into the basement, and is gone.

I stand gaping for just a moment longer before I turn and run up the stairs, hurtling up to the attic. I slam the door shut behind me, then stand with my back to the door, trying to catch my breath.

Then I walk over to my mom's bed, and after hesitating a moment, I shake her awake.

She blinks at me, groggy.

"Mom, there's a ghost downstairs," I whisper.

Mom squints at me, trying to wake up.

"I'm sleeping," she says, annoyed. And then she covers her head with the pillow.

"Mom," I whisper again, shaking her arm, my voice cracking. "Mom, I need your help."

My mom reaches out from under the covers and gently bats me away. "Leave me alone," she says, her voice cold and far away.

After a moment, I hear her breath get steady and even. I step away from the bed and sit down on the floor with my back to the door, watching her sleep, trying to steady my own breathing.

There've been so many times when I've had to do things on my own: comforting myself after nightmares, nursing myself through colds and the flu. One time a raccoon invaded our house, and I had to trap it in a towel and throw it out the front door. Still, it makes me almost breathless, the hurt. I feel starkly alone.

I listen in the dark, but all the noises of the house have gone silent.

I give myself a talking-to:

There's no such thing as ghosts, sweetie, I tell myself. *You've always had an overactive imagination. This is exactly the kind of thing you've decided you don't believe anymore, as of this very night.*

And then, when that doesn't quite work:

If you can just make it to morning, you'll be fine. Ghosts only come at night. I think.

I wish Germ were here. Together we would know what to do. Together it's like we make one fully formed human. I just have to make it to the bus and Germ in the morning, and everything will be okay.

I sit staring out the window all night, until the sky begins to lighten above the horizon. And when the day grows hazy outside, I watch my mom get up from bed and pull on her robe and walk to the door, like a person in a trance. She doesn't see me till she nearly trips over me.

She blinks at me a moment. And then she merely waits for me to get out of her way.

I follow her into the hall and peer downstairs.

The parlor below, the hallway, the kitchen, all seem quiet and normal.

I come to the bottom of the stairs and look at the closed basement door awhile. All normal at first glance.

And then I see the clock hanging in the parlor. I'm going to be late for the bus.

CHAPTER 3

azed, I rush into an oversize sweater and a pair of stretchy pants and two socks that don't match and put my flashlight around my neck. I make a jelly sandwich and hurry back up to the attic to check on Mom, who's already in front of her computer working.

I set the alarm on her computer to remind her to eat. "There's spaghetti in the fridge," I say. "And drink some milk. It's good for you."

I kiss her—a gesture she pulls away from. And then I race outside to the safe harbor of the bus just as it pulls up.

When I see Germ, I let out a breath I didn't know I was holding. Seeing her familiar freckles, her impatient gestures for me to sit down, makes me feel like I'm *safe*, even if she is wearing that goofy eyeliner again, and now lip gloss too.

I plop down next to her as the bus lurches into motion. I'm on the verge of telling her everything that happened last night, when she turns to me.

"I think Eliot Falkor has a stomach virus," she says. "He's not acting like himself. I think he may have a fever. I tried to take his temperature by sticking a thermometer under his armpit, but his armpit isn't really an armpit, you know?"

I do know. Eliot Falkor is Germ's iguana. He doesn't completely have armpits.

Germ continues, talking faster than I can think, with her usual lack of decibel control. "Maybe he picked something up when I took him to the park yesterday. I thought he'd start barfing. I mean, I don't think iguanas barf, but he was *green*. I mean, not the normal green but a *pukey green*. But I read this thing once in *Reptile Enthusiast* . . ."

I glance back at the other kids as they board the bus. Should I interrupt and say something? What if someone overhears?

"Did you watch the news last night, the thing about polar bears?" Germ is obsessed with the news. She lies awake worrying about it, or sometimes stomps around in anger about something she saw. It does seem, even to me, that things on the news are always getting worse.

She talks about polar bears as we pass the immense Seaport Civil War cemetery and Founders Square, which make up the center of our small town. "Sometimes I feel like the world is ending," Germ goes on, and then enumerates why. By the time we get to school, she hasn't paused for breath.

And so, before I know it, we're at school and my secret is still bursting to get out. But in the light of the day, my fears are also beginning to fade a little. The more I look around at kids doing the things they do every day, and the bored face of the bus driver, and the cars converging on the school parking lot like always, the more it feels like last night was a strange dream, and impossible. I guess it feels like ghosts couldn't possibly exist in a world where some kid just threw fish filet all over the front of the bus.

And then, as a last aside as we're walking through the double doors into school, Germ says—a little awkwardly—that she's doing a talent for the Fall Fling with Bibi West on Sunday night, and I nearly fall over my own feet.

Of all the things Germ and I are known for in our

class, the biggest is that once, in second grade, I bit Bibi West because she called Germ "Germ Fartley" instead of her real name, Gemma Bartley. Germ is famous for then promptly adopting the nickname and introducing herself that way from then on. The cruelty of the nickname, though, was not an isolated incident.

Bibi is this complicated combination of cruel and charming. She likes to make up funny dances and do them behind teachers' backs (charming). She gives the people she likes little presents constantly—scented erasers, squishy soft pencil cases, special candy from her trips to Portugal to visit her grandparents (also charming). Once, in third grade, she even handed out lemons to a select few third graders, setting in motion a trend of lemon-giving that lasted several months and worked its way down to the kindergartners. She is the kind of person who can make you want lemons for no reason at all.

On the other hand, she loves to talk about people behind their backs (cruel). And she has a way of finding out people's secrets and using the resulting information like money in the bank.

But recently Bibi—and seemingly everyone else in the sixth grade—has decided she wants to be friends with Germ.

Germ holds funerals for her lunches every day. She likes to run laps around the playground at recess to see if she can beat her previous time. She is blond and freckled and fleshy and restless, proud of her large, round, powerful body when some people seem to think she shouldn't be.

But it feels like she came back from summer vacation with a new kind of air around her, or at least everybody *else* came back different. Because now the loud self-confidence that used to put kids off is something people admire. Kids who used to tease her have started seeking her out. Even the name "Germ" sounds suddenly cool in people's mouths.

The new air has definitely not extended to me. I'm so small and quiet that sometimes people forget I'm there (although, I do have a bit of a kicking-biting streak). I'm ridiculously clumsy and unathletic and always get picked last for teams. I cut my own hair, so my head is kind of a disaster, and that doesn't even come close to my clothes, which are a combination of Mom's old oversize things and the results of a yearly shopping trip I talk my mom into, where she stares into space while I fail at figuring out the rules of coordinating. I barely talk to people I don't know. Even when I make the effort (which is rare), my tongue just freezes in my mouth. Long story short, I tend to fade next to Germ. Although, Germ says that if I'd just share the contents of my brain with the rest of the world, they'd see it's like the ruby slippers from *The Wizard of Oz* in there.

I'd rather keep to myself. But now kids gather around Germ in corners to talk, or laugh, or just linger. I walk into rooms and find Germ sitting with people I don't know, chatting, and it makes my heart pound a lopsided jealous rhythm, because I've never seen Germ look so happy or flattered (and also nervous, tucking her hair every few seconds). And even though I'm really, really scared of the ghost I think I saw (*did* I see it?) last night, the Bibi thing is my worst fears realized.

We make our way to our lockers. I still can't get a word in because Germ is telling me all the details of the Fall Fling excitedly: how Bibi asked her; how the talent they're doing is so secret, she can't even tell me.

And then my chance to speak up comes because Germ pauses to catch her breath. And instead of my telling her about the ghost, something else entirely comes out.

"But, it's *Bibi*," I say. Germ gives me a sideways, wary look as I falter on. "Remember when she used to chase Muffintop the stray cat around the parking lot, trying to step on his tail? Remember when she used to call Matt Schnibble 'Freckly Little Schnibbles' and make him cry?"

Germ gets quiet. "She's not like that anymore," she says, uncertain and a little annoyed at the same time. Her freckles stand out on her cheeks as they flush. "She was going through a hard time then. She was really insecure. She's not that bad."

I don't reply. Something about the way she defends Bibi, like they've had deep talks, makes me shut up like a clam. For the moment, my thoughts of the ghost have flown to the back of my head. I don't blame Bibi for wanting to be friends with Germ. Germ is bottled lightning; Germ is the most likable person I know. But my feelings are swirling a million miles a minute and . . .

"Bibi will be good, but I'm gonna be terrible," Germ says. "They're gonna spitball me."

I think this is probably true, so I try to be helpful.

"Just make sure you don't wear eyeliner," I blurt out. It's like the words just escape my mouth before I've really thought about them.

Germ is silent for a moment, blinking at me. "I *like* eyeliner."

"I know. It's just, it's not very, um, *you*," I muddle out, biting my tongue.

"I can like new things," Germ says quietly.

I nod silently.

We get to our lockers. I unpack the lunch I made, and scribble a quick note to myself on my lunch bag before putting it into my locker. (I write poems to myself on my lunch bag every day in my mom's handwriting so that people will think my mom is really loving and no one will think I'm being neglected. Probably 89 percent of the energy I spend at school is on making it look like everything is normal at home so no one will ever have a reason to take me away.)

D'quan Daniels, who Germ used to crush on in fourth grade, passes us and waves at Germ, who picks at her hair before waving back. He looks at me as if he might wave to me, too, but then quickly breaks eye contact. Some of the boys are scared of me because last year I kicked a kid in the shins when he tried to tackle me in keep-away.

Germ, blushing with a combination of self-consciousness and pride, watches him walk away. It's a look she wears more and more, and I don't like it. Germ has never cared what people think, but these days she seems to care a lot.

Still, as her eyes catch mine, she suddenly zeroes in on me. She cocks her head, looking at me and placing a hand on her hip, her annoyance with me gone.

"Are you okay?" she asks. "You look kind of off."

"I'm fine," I say nervously, now unsure how to tell her about last night, or even if I want to. "I didn't get much sleep."

Germ folds her arms, unconvinced.

"What's going on with you?" she asks sharply. "Tell me." Now that she's focused on me, she reads me like a book.

I look around the crowded hall. Everyone is busy talking, laughing. My throat tickles with nerves. I suddenly feel ridiculous.

But I lean forward and tell her anyway.

"I think I saw a ghost last night," I say, low, feeling my face flush.

I wait for Germ to laugh, or be annoyed, or both, as she looks at me for a long moment. Sometimes I worry that she is losing that strange, wild, fighting-spirit piece of herself that makes us fit together so perfectly.

But now she lets out a breath decisively.

"I'll ask my mom if I can sleep over," she says.

CHAPTER 4

We go over it all several times on the bus ride home: the sound of muttering in the hall, the glowing man hovering by the door of the basement. Germ makes me slow down over this or that detail now and then, but she never laughs. She looks uncertain but not amused.

"Nobody's gonna believe you," she says, ruminating. "And your mom won't be any help, no offense." She gives me an apologetic smile. "I guess the first thing we have to do is see if he's there again tonight."

"And then what?" I wonder aloud.

Germ stares out the window, thinking. "On *Los Angeles Pet Psychic* they got rid of a bad spirit by burning something called a smudge stick all around the house. It had, like, oregano in it or something."

I blink at her. *Los Angeles Pet Psychic* is one of her favorite shows. She's always waiting for them to do a segment on an iguana, but it has never panned out. Still, I doubt how much burning oregano could help if I do end up seeing a ghost again.

Walking into the house, I see that half the groceries I ordered online earlier this week are scattered on the counter: eight of the same Swanson frozen dinners, four boxes of Pop-Tarts, four frozen pizzas, a box of spaghetti, eight cans of soup. There's a whole bag full of candy— Twizzlers and caramels and all sorts of treats I order too because my mom doesn't care.

Some of the bags have been unpacked, but it looks like Mom got halfway through and then forgot and moved on to something else. Even after all these years being friends with Germ, I flush with embarrassment. But Germ briskly crosses the kitchen and starts putting things away as if it's the most normal thing in the world, and I help her, gratefully.

After we finish, we find Mom upstairs in her attic room, staring out the window at the sea, as she does for hours every evening. The pull to the ocean and this window view of it is so strong, she starts muttering nervously to herself whenever she has to leave the house, and we always have to hurry home.

"Hey, Mrs. Oaks," Germ says, behind me in the doorway.

"He's out there swimming," Mom says automatically, her eyes on the sea.

"Yeah," Germ says, turning a kind smile to me. "His legs must be tired." Germ reaches out and gives my arm a squeeze. I know she feels bad for me, but she also tries to be funny about it. I think she understands that you only have the mom you have.

"Germ's sleeping over," I say. "And I have some progress reports I need you to sign." My progress reports always have some variation of the same note at the bottom: *Rosie is very bright but doesn't speak very often. Rosie daydreams too much.* I know my mom will sign them without reading them.

Mom gives a vague smile to both of us. "That's nice," she says, and then looks away from us in silence.

Outside, the sun is low and distant in the cloudy sky. Dusk will be here quickly, and Germ and I have both agreed that night is the best time, probably the only time, to see a ghost. Germ has to get home at the crack of dawn tomorrow for soccer practice.

"I guess we should get online and find out everything we can about warding off spirits," I say. Germ nods.

"If we even see any spirits," she adds, to manage expectations.

So we spend the next hours digging up information on charms and ghost repellents (ghosts don't like silver, apparently) and exorcisms. Since exorcisms need a priest, and we don't know any priests, we get a bunch of silver spoons from the kitchen and hang them from strings on doorknobs and wall hooks, making do with what we have.

In my room, Germ goes to my closet to get the spare pajamas she keeps on hand, and notices that my stories are missing from where they're usually piled up on the floor. She turns to me quizzically.

"I burned them," I say nonchalantly. "I'm finished with stories." Her eyes widen significantly, but she doesn't say anything. Tact is not really her strong suit, but sometimes even Germ knows when to keep her thoughts to herself.

"Now what?" she says.

"Now we station ourselves at the basement door. And wait, I guess."

"You know you get low blood sugar," Germ says. "You're gonna need some snacks."

In the living room, in a fort we have built from pillows, Germ and I sit and stare at the basement door while eating Little Debbie cakes and Twizzlers, and wait, our legs up the wall beside each other. We are having a burping contest, which is hopeless on my end, given Germ's innate gift for burping. As the sun gets lower on the horizon, I grow more and more nervous, chomping the Twizzlers so hard that my teeth clack together, and even Germ has to tell me to slow down or I'll go into a sugar coma.

Mom drifts through at one point and nearly trips over us. She stares down at us in surprise.

"What are you doing here?" she asks. And I wonder if she means here on the floor or in her life in general.

"We're trying to see a ghost," I say.

Mom nods as if I've said we're doing our taxes, and circles past us to get a snack from the kitchen. Germ shrugs at me.

After a couple of hours we start to get bored. Eventually my mom goes to bed—I listen to her familiar shuffling tread in the hallways above, as if she doesn't know quite where she's going until she ends up there. We lie with our feet up the side of the parlor couch.

"Do you think D'quan or Andrew Silva is cuter?" asks Germ. Germ is increasingly boy crazy. To me, boys seem as uninteresting as they always have.

We wait. And wait and wait. In fact, we wait for half the night, long past midnight, and no ghost appears. No creaking, no booing, nothing. We watch part of a PG-13 movie that Germ's not allowed to watch. We wait because we want to see something, but also, we're afraid to go to sleep. Eventually we do sleep, though, me lying in one direction in the fort and Germ the other.

I only stir when I hear the whispering. For a moment, I can't move. I slide my eyes to the clock. It's two a.m.

"Hate her," the voice rasps. It's coming from the direction of the basement.

My body goes hot and cold. My heart thrums, my stomach drops like a roller coaster, a heaviness and coldness comes over me.

I nudge Germ with just the slightest movement, and feel her stir awake.

Slowly we sit up, facing each other.

"Do you hear that?" I mouth silently to Germ. She looks at me, head cocked, then shakes her head.

"My house," the voice says. It gets louder. I wait for Germ to acknowledge it, but she only gazes at me with wide, confused eyes.

We move slowly to the entrance to our fort, and crawl halfway out. I stare at the basement door.

There's no doubt; the voice is coming from behind it. And there is a glow. And as the voice gets closer, as if its owner is climbing the stairs, the glow gets brighter.

I can feel my hands begin to tremble.

"Rosie, what is it?" Germ whispers. "Are you okay?"

"You can't hear it? Really?" I whisper, low.

She shakes her head again. But instead of looking like she doubts me, she appears to listen harder. I'm panicked. I *need* Germ to hear it. I need to know I'm not crazy, at least.

"Never tell, never tell," the voice says, growing ever closer.

Germ looks to be straining her ears with all her might, though the voice is as loud and clear as day. I reach for her hand, terrified, and squeeze it tight.

"Serves them right."

At that moment, Germ's eyes widen.

"I hear it," she mouths. But she's straining, even though the voice is loud by now.

I point to the door, to the glow coming from under the crack.

Germ stares hard at it. She squeezes my fingers harder. And then the glow flares, as if in anger. And we both jump, and Germ grasps my sleeve.

"I see it," she whispers.

We both cower in the blankets, facing the door, clutching the spoons we've hung around our necks.

"The yellow-haired one is never quiet," the voice says suddenly, suspiciously. Its owner has reached the top of the stairs, just on the other side of the door. He knows we're here.

And then Germ, for some reason, startles and looks over my shoulder, not toward the basement door but over the top of the fort, and slowly she stands.

"Um, Rosie?" she says, not whispering anymore. "What does a ghost look like, exactly?" She sounds sick, panicked.

"Like, um, dead and see-through-ish," I whisper back, eyes glued to the basement door, thinking, *Everyone knows what a ghost looks like.*

"Um. Rosie?"

"Yeah."

"I think there's more than one."

I notice now, what she's talking about, and I feel sick with fright. The glow isn't only coming from in front of us, but all around us.

I swivel, slowly.

A woman stands in the parlor staring at us, a ball of yarn in her hands. A man is just behind her wearing a yellow rain slicker, sopping wet and pale, starfishes stuck to his arms. There is another woman by the couch, very old, all in white. And closest—just inches from us—is a boy with floppy brown hair and a dour expression, like he's just tasted something rotten. He's a dreadful sight: maybe thirteen or fourteen, wide brown eyes, a furrowed forehead, pale, his dark hair plastered wetly down around his ears, bluish skin. He glows with a bluish light that casts a dim glow onto the wall behind him.

We're surrounded.

CHAPTER 5

The boy raises one finger and points at me, frowning. My heart pounds in my fingers, my feet, my ears.

"You," he says, "can see us?" His voice is as clear as a bell, like a real living boy talking to us, but there's nothing living about him—he's pale and limp, a shadow of a person who looks half-drowned.

I swallow, and nod.

He stares at me for a long moment, and then he seems to crumple into himself, hanging his head and shaking it. "No," he says. "No, no, no."

Germ and I gape at him, exchanging a look of confusion and fear. I don't know what to say, or if I should say anything, or if we should run. I eye the silver spoons we've dangled all over the room. Whatever they are supposed to do, they are not doing it.

The boy looks Germ up and down, uncertainly. Her face is pale white, her freckles drained. "You see me too?"

She hesitates for a moment, then nods furiously.

The boy lets out a long, slow sigh, his eyes full of sadness. "Well, I guess you've really done it now," he finally says. Germ and I exchange another confused look.

Then a voice behind us makes us leap. *"Done it now!"*

I swirl around to see the man I saw last night, who is now standing on the landing on this side of the basement door. He grins at me, then lets out a loud, mad peal of laughter. "Danger now. So much danger now." He laughs again. I flinch at each barking sound, but try to steady myself. His eyes glow like coals as he glares at me, full of hatred.

The dead boy floats up beside me and glowers at the man.

"Don't worry about *the Murderer*," he says. "He's harmless." But then he pauses, and appears to rethink his words, because he adds, "I mean, everybody does call him 'the Murderer,' and he *does* want to murder you, and he's pretty territorial. But it's not your fault."

The boy reaches an arm toward me. I leap back and let out a small scream, but not before his arm has sliced right through me—with no effect, just the faintest feeling of a cool breeze running through my stomach. "See? He can't touch you. None of us can." He frowns, and glances at the man—the Murderer—again. "Still, don't go into the basement at night. Some ghosts do sometimes figure out . . . alternatives."

Germ and I are both too scared to respond. There are too many questions swirling in my head, and my heart is beating too hard for me to speak.

The other ghosts hover around us, staring at us intently. I try to steady my breath enough to settle on one question, the one that burns the most. "What are you doing here?" I manage to whisper. It sounds more like a croak.

The boy looks at me a long moment. "We're *always* here. We've been here your whole life. I'm Ebb," the boy says. He looks around the room, his mournful eyes wide, as if deciding something. "Well," he finally says, resigned, "I guess you'd both better come with me."

He begins moving toward the stairs, and casts a dark, strained look back at us. "If you could keep up, I'd appreciate it."

Germ and I eye each other, bewildered.

Ebb pauses at the landing, then floats halfway through the banister toward us. "Night won't last forever," he says, "and we disappear at dawn."

Germ looks to me, her eyes questioning if we should follow. I shake my head uncertainly.

"You couldn't have always been here," I make myself brave enough to say. "This is impossible."

Ebb sighs, hovering impatiently.

"I was afraid of it happening when I watched you burn your stories."

I give a small start. The thought of being watched the other night prickles my skin all over, makes me sick to my stomach.

"I guess you've given up on writing them," Ebb continues. "It happens all the time; people give up on fanciful things as they get older. But for people like you, from a family like yours . . . If you push magic away in one place, it will find you in another. I think probably when you burned your stories"—he pauses, trying to think of how to explain—"you closed a door and opened a window. And that window is *the sight*."

"The sight?" I whisper.

Ebb shakes his head, as if we are wasting time. "It's

how you can see me now, all of a sudden. You must have triggered your sight."

I'm still trying to grasp what he's saying, when Germ says nervously, "What about me? What triggered *my* sight?"

But Ebb only floats up the stairs, pausing in the upper hallway at the top, staring darkly down at us. He floats back and forth, as if pacing.

"It's very important that you come," he insists. "There are things I need to show you."

I nod to Germ. As dour as the dead boy looks, I don't think he wants to hurt us. We move toward the stairs, though slowly.

When we reach him at the top, he pivots and continues down the hall.

He leads us down the hallway and stops in front of the antique dresser tucked into a nook by a small, octagonal window looking out onto the yard. With pretty turquoise handles and lovingly carved inlays, the dresser has always seemed—like so many things—as if it belonged to someone I don't know, instead of to my mom. Now Ebb looks down at the floor just in front of it, nervous, uncertain. He glances up at me.

Upstairs in the attic, I hear my mom's bed creak. No

footsteps, but it sounds like she's stirring. We all wait silently. Finally, all settles again.

Ebb stares down at the floor, then at us, as if we're supposed to know what to do.

"Um," Germ says.

Ebb, exasperated, sighs and rolls his eyes. I'm beginning to notice he sighs a lot.

"You'll need to move the dresser. I can't exactly do it myself." He pushes his arm into a wall and pulls it out again as if to demonstrate.

Haltingly, Germ and I sidle up beside each other, then gently lean into the dresser from the right side so that it slides to the left.

I turn my gaze again to the floor. There's a gap between two of the boards, only noticeable if you are looking straight at it. I kneel slowly and tuck a fingernail into one of the tiny crevices and pull. To my amazement, the board comes up easily. My heart, already thrumming, begins to skip and flutter.

There's a small, dark space here. I grasp my flashlight from around my neck and shine it in. Spiders scatter in the beam of light, and dust whorls fly up around me; the hole smells like old wood and paper, and my light strobes across a shape, rectangular and dusty.

I reach in to pull it out.

It's a book, square and worn, leather bound. On the cover someone has etched an illustration of the earth, with figures in the space surrounding it: men and women, each one with a malicious, angry face. These figures seem to be casting threads from their hands that weave around the world. In the upper right-hand corner is the moon, and a tiny figure standing on its surface with her back turned, tears flying into the air around her head.

It's a strange and disturbing etching. And at the top, in familiar handwriting, are the words "The Witch Hunter's Guide to the Universe."

"My mother etched this," I say.

Ebb nods. "She hid this here, before you were born. She wanted to keep it close without you ever seeing it. Then she"—he looks at me apologetically—"forgot."

"Forgot?" Germ asks.

He hesitates. "Forgot everything," he says, his eyes flashing down at mine for a moment, before flashing away. "At least everything that matters. Once they took it all away from her."

I feel a creeping, sick feeling. Like I have known something bone-deep all my life but no one has ever named it until now: that there is something really wrong with my mom. Something beyond what a doctor could say.

"*They?*" I ask.

Ebb looks down at me for a long time, hesitant. "There are worse things in the world than ghosts in the basement, Rosie," he says. "You'll need to know about them now if you want to live."

CHAPTER 6

In second grade, I stopped talking for a whole month. It just seemed like every day I said less and less until it was whittled down to zero. Germ said it was my quiet way of yelling for help.

At home, my mom didn't mind or notice, and when my teachers asked her about it, she said vaguely that the doctor was helping, and when my doctor asked about it, she said the teachers were helping, but neither thing was true.

Germ minded a lot. She tried to coax me into talking by waving my favorite candy in my face but telling me

I had to ask for it. I didn't budge. So she started talking through all the silences. She talked more so I could talk less. It felt like she was carrying all the words for me that I couldn't say.

And then, in the middle of some facts she was telling me about her bike one day, she stopped and took a deep breath and said, "Rosie, tomorrow, things are going to change. You are gonna say good morning to me, and then ask me some things, and that'll be the end of it. It's time to rejoin the world."

It was an overwhelming feeling, to know that the next day I would have to talk again and try to act like a normal person in the world, again. I wanted it and I didn't want it at the same time.

Holding the book with my mother's writing on it, I have a similar feeling. A feeling of moving toward something I'm not sure I can face.

I sit on the floor. My hands shake as I grasp *The Witch Hunter's Guide to the Universe,* and open it. And then flip through its pages.

It's not a very thick book, but the pages are dense—full of drawings and tight, cramped notes.

And witches. It is a book full of them. Over the next twenty-six pages are profiles of thirteen witches—some harmless-looking, some clearly malicious. For each witch there are descriptions on the right-hand page, written in all sorts of different handwriting, some very faded, as if different people have undertaken to write the notes over the years. But for each witch there's a drawing on the left-hand page created by my mother.

The witches are beautifully drawn, shaded with charcoal. Some wear wild clothes, grimacing or sticking out their tongues; others have quiet faces with murderers' eyes. There's a picture of a greenish-tinted witch clutching a bag of gold tightly to his chest. There's a tall man in a suit with his hand on the back of a wolf, a woman with a necklace of watches, and a bearded man holding a handful of spiders (though his picture has a big *X* through it). They have names like the Greedy Man, Hypocriffa, the Griever, Babble, Miss Rage, Chaos, Convenia, Mable the Mad, the Trapper. In my mom's skillful hands, they look as real as someone you might see on the street, only monstrous—with evil in their eyes, and mouths that smile with malice.

I keep flipping until I reach a drawing that makes my hands freeze. It's a woman staring out at me in desperation, dark black circles around her green eyes. She's covered in webs, and moths and caterpillars—perched on her shoulders, clinging to her sleeves, and entangled in her hair. Her face, as scary as it is, is *nondescript somehow*, the kind of face you might see a hundred times and still never manage to recognize. My mom has spent a lot of time, probably the most time, on this one. It's the most complete.

But it's the description that has frozen my hands. My mom has underlined the words again and again in several spots.

The Memory Thief: Weakest of the thirteen witches.

Curse: The removal and hoarding of memories. Forgetful herself, this witch covets the memories of others.

Skills: Keen sense of navigation, direction, and smell. Sees ultraviolet, sees in the dark. Sensitive to the slightest movement.

Familiars: Her moths are her weapons and her spies. They spread out all over the world at night and steal from her victims. They can be distinguished by the shifting, sparkling

*patterns on their wings, which are actually
the shifting dust of the memories they have
stolen.*

*Victims: A person cursed by the Memory
Thief may appear normal, go about their
normal lives, but they've lost memories
of the past, of the people they are close to,
even how to love others. At times, entire
towns have lost their histories to this
terrible witch.*

I feel sick as I read these words. I stare at the moths in the drawing, tracing them with my fingers.

I move through the rest of the pages faster, skimming through the varied handwriting, squinting at some pages yellowed with age or stains. There are labeled sections:

"The Invisible World and Its Beings"
"The Oakses and Their Weapons"
"Legends"
"Secrets of the Earth and Moon"
"What Is a Witch?"

At the last section, which is written in my mom's unmistakable handwriting, I pause again and read:

There are moments in life when we hear about something so terrible, it feels as if we've been punched in the stomach. That feeling—that sense of despair—is a witch's greatest thrill; it is like the air she breathes.

Witches are made of the darkest shades of a hidden and invisible fabric that permeates the world. Like ghosts, most people can't see them. However, they contain just a hint of the physical world too, and so they are sturdier and far more powerful than other magical beings. While they can't walk through walls like ghosts can (they're too solid), they can open doors and windows with a flick of the wrist, make small items float in the air. They control great multitudes of familiars—half-magical, half-real creatures just like them—who do their bidding.

Witches are not solid enough to kill, but they are excellent thieves. They're known to steal and hoard anything they can get their hands on: jewelry right off of human necks, favorite mementos, socks, even the odd pet. They steal for the sake of taking what is ours and what we care about: to keep it for themselves, but most importantly to make us feel the loss of it. Most of all, witches steal the good things inside us. What's inside us is the thing they want most. That's where their curses come in.

To lay a curse, a witch must touch her victim, as if laying a scent. Her familiars do the rest: gathering the good things she means to pillage—memories, time, wisdom, and so on. Each witch treasures a different prize.

By stealing what is good in us, the witches leave voids behind. And humans full of voids lose all the things that matter: hope, connection, love. They lose even the vaguest whispers in their hearts that there is magic and beauty in the universe. By cursing as many victims as they can and stealing all the good, the witches hope to capture the world in a web of despair so thick that it reflects only the ugliness of

their misshapen hearts. In such a world,
their power will be boundless.

But witches do have their limits. They
can float but not fly (though sometimes
winged familiars can help). They cannot be
two places at once, or disappear from one
place and reappear in another. And most
of all, because moonlight has hope in it,
witches cannot tolerate it. It burns them.
This means they choose only to travel the
world and lay their curses at the dark moon,
when the moon reflects no light at all.

What's more, witches are not all-knowing
or all-seeing, and they rely on their familiars
as messengers and spies to find the things
they seek.

This is how they've always found witch
hunters. It is how they will find me.

I turn the page, but the rest of the book is blank. This is
where the guide ends, with my mother talking about how
she will be found.

I lay the book down, still open, and reach my arms
around myself. I look up at Ebb.

"Is this all real?" I whisper. "Are these witches"—I nod to the book—"real?"

Ebb nods. "As real as I am. The women in your family have kept track in this book. They've kept everything they could learn about witches in one place."

The three of us sit in silence for a long time, as I try to make sense of what he's saying. I stare down at the last page again. *This is how they will find me.*

I touch the words, trying to touch my mom's old self that wrote them.

"They found her?" I ask.

He nods solemnly.

"Yes." He clears his throat. "Witches don't take kindly to those who hunt them." He avoids my eyes.

I take this in for a few moments, a strange, sea-urchin feeling prickling in my chest. I gather my breath. "*Hunt* them?" I finally ask.

Ebb nods, and his expression is unreadable.

"You come from a long line of witch hunters, Rosie," he says. "And your mom is the last known witch hunter alive."

CHAPTER 7

"My mom's not a witch hunter. She's a data entry specialist," I say.

My stomach churns hotly. Beyond the octagonal window, the thick sliver of moon darts out from behind a cloud for a moment and then dims.

"This isn't true. None of this is true," I say. "There are no witches. I've given up believing things like this." There has to be an explanation for all of it: dreaming, hallucinating, a bad sloppy joe at school. I wait for Ebb to evaporate the way dreams do when you realize you're in one.

But Ebb only looks back and forth between me and Germ, as if he's deciding something against his better judgment.

"I can show you something more. I think it would convince you about witches and everything else," he says. "*But* you'd have to promise me that you'd both do as I say. Even the witch's familiars—as mindless as they are—might notice Rosie now that . . ."

"Now that what?" Germ asks for me as I hesitate.

"The sight changes you. It's an extra sense, and witches and their familiars can pick up on it like a light in the dark."

Germ swivels her head, studying me as if looking for the change.

Glancing out the window at the height of the moon, Ebb floats backward.

"It's about time for them to arrive," he says. He turns toward the stairs to the attic, then suddenly pivots back to us.

"You can't disturb what's happening. You can't meddle in any way. Promise me that you won't. You couldn't stop it if you tried, anyhow."

"We promise. But stop what?" I ask. And I hear my voice teetering.

He turns reluctantly to the stairs. "Your mom's curse. Are you coming?"

Ebb nods to us, then floats up the stairs and through the door of my mom's attic room. I follow with Germ at my heels, take the knob, hold my breath, and open the door slowly.

My mom is sleeping peacefully. The moon peeps out again from behind the clouds, then disappears behind the overcast sky. Nothing strange, nothing out of place.

Ebb ushers us into the closet, then drifts in behind us and nods to Germ to close the door. It's slatted, so we can see out, though it's harder to see in. I used to hide in here when I was little, watching my mom, trying to figure her out.

"We're safe here," Ebb whispers. "They're mindless creatures, like I said. Your sight's the only reason we even have to hide at all. And they won't look for us or notice us if we stay quiet and hidden."

"'They' who?" Germ asks. But Ebb is intently watching through the slats now, staring in the direction of the attic window, and he doesn't answer.

We follow his gaze and wait. For several minutes, nothing happens and nothing comes. And then Ebb raises an arm slowly, extending a finger to point at something beyond the window.

In the distance, a strange shape is making its way toward us over the ocean, like a ribbon threaded through the air. Whatever it is, it's made of the same diaphanous glowing stuff as Ebb, and moving fast. Before long, it's close enough that I can see it's not *one* shape but a cluster of smaller ones—hundreds of tiny, glowing silhouettes fluttering and flapping in the breeze.

"What are those?" Germ whispers.

"Moths," I breathe, a feeling like rocks in my stomach, remembering the page from *The Witch Hunter's Guide to the Universe*, the picture my mother drew.

"The moths and what they carry are deeply precious to the Memory Thief," Ebb says, "like a collection of jewels she hoards away. There are billions of them, I imagine. Far too many for her to ever even notice. But it doesn't matter; her greed for what they steal is limitless. They come here like clockwork every night to collect. Ever since the night your mom was cursed."

The shapes get closer and closer. The moonlight glints off their wings, which undulate with color. The first few arrive at the attic window like in an air ballet—graceful, delicate.

"They're gonna hit the window," Germ says, but as these

words leave her lips, the shapes gather along the bottom of the windowsill. The window creaks open as if they are lifting it, and the first of the moths flutter into the room.

They're unlike any moths I've ever seen. Some are purple in the moonlight; some glow yellow and white. The patterns of sparkling, iridescent dust on their tiny wings move and change.

The creatures land gently on my mother's bed. They crawl and flutter over her shape under her blankets. As they do, they seem to brighten and change color, as if they are taking something from my mother that charges their wings like batteries.

I feel my skin go cold. And it sinks in that this is not a dream, because in dreams things do not really hurt. But it hurts to watch this, because I know exactly what's happening, as clear as day. They're stealing everything that should make my mom love me. All the memories that add up to someone's love. I feel the loss of it, watching them. All the things that have been taken.

Beside me, I see recognition crossing Germ's face. First comes the look of shock, then sadness. Then a familiar kind of anger.

I see what she's going to do a moment before she does it.

She can't help it. Germ has always been my protector like I've always been hers.

Her fists are tight. Her face is clenched. She coils back.

"No!" I hiss, reaching for her—but it's too late. She springs toward the closet door, knocking me forward, and we both tumble into the room.

Germ lunges toward my mom's bed and slaps at the moths. Ebb zips forward as if to stop her, but falls right through her.

The moths scatter, and circle around our heads, once, twice, three times, as if sizing us up. Then they race toward the window—out, and up and away.

Germ freezes. My mom tosses in her sleep and lets out a small moan, but does not wake.

Ebb zips closer to the window and looks out, then back at me. "They must have picked up on Rosie's sight," he says. "That's why they left so fast. A girl with the sight, in the house of a witch hunter." He shoots a glare at Germ.

Germ looks wild-eyed and ashamed all at once. "I'm sorry. I just . . ."

But Ebb turns away from her and watches the sky, his face tight and fearful. Minutes pass; we wait—for what, I don't know. Time moves slowly, but nothing happens. The sliver of moon pokes out of the clouds again and illuminates the room.

Ebb's shoulders seem to relax a bit. He turns and looks at us. "I should never have shown you," he says.

The way he says it lets me breathe a little easier. Like whatever he's afraid of is not coming.

But then there is the smallest shift in the breeze. Clouds cross over the moon and linger there, and we are engulfed in darkness.

A moment later—somewhere outside and over the ocean, far away but unmistakable—a distant shriek carries across the air.

Ebb turns back to the window, tilting his head, listening. "Maybe it has nothing to do with us," he whispers. "Maybe . . ."

The wind begins to blow.

The ghost in the yellow rain slicker bursts through the wall in a panic. Noticing us, he whispers, "Hide," and then zips through the opposite wall and out of sight.

Fog is rolling in thickly off the sea. On the air, I hear what sounds like the softest of whispers—so soft, I think I'm imagining it. "Tricked?" the whisper says, far away but also, somehow, close, and as ancient-feeling as dust.

"Back in the closet," Ebb whispers, and Germ lurches for the slatted doors as I step back.

"My mom," I whisper, moving to grab her arms.

Ebb floats in front of me and hisses, "There's nothing left for the Memory Thief to take from your mom but you. You've got to hide."

I feel Germ grab the back of my shirt and pull me backward.

Into the closet we stumble, Germ closing the door behind us with her free hand. Ebb zips through the door and settles beside us.

Just as we settle, I hear it. The sound of the window sliding open again.

Beside me, Ebb is dim and trembling. The thought crosses my mind that he should have nothing to fear since he's dead, but all thoughts flee at the sound of rustling outside the window, a sound like thick silky fabric rustling. Germ gently grasps the inner edges of the door as if to secure it with her bare hands.

I press my face close to the slats and peer through them.

With the moon gone, it's almost black, but I can just see the outlines of a figure in a dark dress moving about the room, looking all around it as if for something it has lost. I can't see the figure's face, but I can hear her sniffing the air. She flits through the dark carefully, softly—stopping to study and sniff this and that. She reminds me of some animal, and after a moment I realize it's an insect, a moth—fluttering and feeling her way along. She moves to the foot of the bed, where my mom still sleeps.

I take a breath, and for a moment the figure pauses, swiveling slightly toward me, listening. Ebb shakes his head at me, and I hold my breath.

Eventually the woman turns back to my mother.

She speaks, in the same dusty voice of the whisper from the air.

"Annabelle Oaks, how long has it been? Ten years, eleven? It's good to see you after all this time. You do look much changed, much less lively. But . . . have you been hiding something from me? Something my moths have seen?"

Her voice is full of controlled rage and something else: longing, loneliness. She studies my mom asleep in the bed, clearly thinking.

And then she turns and begins to sniff around the room again.

"I do smell a child," she whispers. "Or is it something burning? I can't tell."

She listens, sniffs, and my heart is nearly bursting out of my chest.

"It's not possible. We took . . . ," she says, and is silent for a few moments. "Unless . . ."

And then she makes her way over to the wall to the side of the closet, putting her hands on it.

"Did you cheat me? Is there a child here?" she asks. "A *hidden* child? A girl child?"

Germ reaches for my fingers and squeezes them tight. I don't know if it's to comfort herself or me or both. The woman moves away from the wall, and I silently let out a breath.

And then suddenly a face appears up against the slats. The woman has crept up to the doors and now she's peering in.

Green, sad, empty eyes meet mine. A pale gaunt face. A slim snake of a smile spreads across the woman's lips. Germ grips the doors tight, hopelessly, while I stay glued to the slats, unable to move, paralyzed.

"Come out, come out. I won't hurt you," the woman says, her eyes going from me to Germ and back. A cloud of moths rises from behind her and toward the slats of the door, landing and crawling on them. The slats start to creak, coming loose from their grooves.

Despite myself, I let out a small moan. There's nothing to keep her from us. As more and more moths gather, the slats begin to pull away. Germ lets go of the doors and grips my arm.

But at that moment, there is another change in the room. At the back of my mind I register it: the clouds shift. Moonlight, sudden and bright, floods in on us. The witch—inches from me—startles, and turns. She shrieks, then floats to the window. Pausing for just a moment, crouched on the sill, she turns back to look at us.

"Watch for me at the dark moon, child," she calls over her shoulder. "At the dark moon, I'll end you."

And then, moths gathering around her, she falls out of the window, and is gone.

CHAPTER 8

We wait for several minutes, but nothing happens. The house lies still around us; the moonlight remains bright through the windows. And then the man from downstairs, the one in the rain slicker, floats into the room, muttering to himself. "Scare of my afterlife," he says. "Never been that close."

I feel sick, and Germ looks mortified. Ebb turns to glare at her.

"Half an hour of *seeing*, and look what you two have

done," he says, pulling at his hair in agitation. "This is the worst thing that could have possibly happened."

"I'm sorry," Germ whispers.

There is a long silence as Ebb glowers at Germ, then me. "I should have never shown you," he says, shaking his head. "I'm so stupid."

Germ can't stand anyone putting themselves down, so she reaches out for Ebb's hand, and her fingers slip right through his. "Don't say that," she whispers. "Never say that."

I can only think back to the witch, her eyes on mine, the things she said. *Tricked. A hidden child. A girl child. End you.*

Ebb waves off Germ's attempt at kindness, angry and cold-eyed. "All I know is, if the clouds hadn't moved, if the moon hadn't come out, you'd be . . ."

"The moon?"

"She didn't want to get burned," he says curtly. And then I remember what *The Witch Hunter's Guide* said about this, why witches fear the moonlight.

Then he changes tack again, filled with too many thoughts at once. "She means what she says. When the moon is at its darkest phase, she'll come back for you. She'll punish us ghosts for knowing about you. We're all in terrible danger now."

"When does the moon go dark?" Germ asks.

Ebb stares out at the sky, counting to himself on trembling fingers, his eyebrows low over his eyes. "Dark moon is Wednesday night. Four days," he says.

"Four *days*?" Germ puffs, shocked.

I'm trying to make sense of it. Less than an hour ago I didn't even know witches existed, and now one is coming for me? In four days?

But Ebb is too distracted to respond. He's pacing, in a ghostly way, floating back and forth across the room, dim and drained-looking.

"You should run, leave here tonight." Then he seems to reconsider. "No, it won't be enough. You won't survive on your own. Now that you have the sight, you're a bright target; she'll find you. I know witch curses can't kill, but when she says she'll end you, she means it. You'll need help to get away."

Germ looks at me, guilt written all over her face. Lost for words, I shake my head at her and give her a well-meaning wince. I know she was only trying to fight for me and my mom.

Ebb looks down at his floating feet, thinking. "We need to talk to someone who knows more than I do," he finally says decisively, moving toward the hallway. "I have an idea. Come on. I'll take you. It's not that far away."

"Far away as in we're going out*side*?" Germ says. "Ummm, no. There's, like, a witch out there."

"Trust me, these walls mean nothing to a witch—locks, doors, windows—none of it. If she wants to come for you, she will."

I don't want to follow either, but without a moment's delay, Ebb floats through the wall and disappears. Through the window, I see him floating out into the yard and looking impatient.

I take a deep breath, let it out, and then we walk into the hall and down the stairs.

There is only one ghost in the parlor when we get there. I stop short, chills spilling down my back.

"Fool child," the one Ebb called the Murderer says to me. Germ and I stop in our tracks. He floats slowly closer, his eyes—red like coals—boring into me. They're the eyes of someone who would happily squeeze my life away with his bare hands if he could. I see now there is a red rash around his neck, as if made by a rope. "After what was lost to hide you."

I swallow the lump in my throat. "What do you . . . ?"

But the Murderer doesn't let me finish. "Nevertell, nevertell, nevertell," he whispers. "Never, never, never." His smile drops off his face and he glares at me. And then he floats across the hall, through the basement door, and is gone.

Stepping out onto the front lawn, I shiver. Germ has pulled on her coat, but I've forgotten mine and I instantly regret it. Still, Ebb is already halfway across the yard, and it's all we can do to keep up. My attention is so glued to his back, trying not to lose him, that I don't notice what surrounds us until Germ jerks to a sudden stop beside me, grabbing my arm.

"Rosie," she says. I look back at her impatiently. She's staring out across the lawn toward the sea, and after a moment I follow her gaze, and gasp.

Everything is different.

Far above us, where there was only sky before, is a distant and beautiful pink haze circling the outermost edges of the atmosphere between us and the stars, like the rings around Saturn. Beneath it, distant figures—made of white mist—move amongst the clouds like bees moving from flower to flower. I can't quite make them out—they seem to change shape as they move—one moment becoming part of a cloud, another moment appearing to push clouds along ahead of them. Out on the ocean far beneath the sky, transparent ships float far away, projections of luminous light on the dark water.

It all takes my breath away. It's strange, and frightening, but most of all, it's beautiful.

Beside me, Germ's standing with her mouth hanging open.

"Um, can you please hurry?" We turn to see that Ebb has doubled back, and he looks more miserable than ever, if that's possible. A few ghosts float in and out of the woods behind him, barely noticing us, including an elderly lady in the moonlit yard moving back and forth as if hanging something on a clothesline.

Ebb follows my gaze out to the ocean and the sky. "Oh. Now that you have your *sight*, you'll start to see everything. The world as it really is, all the terrible and wonderful things just under the surface. It's all part of the invisible fabric—that's what witches and ghosts and all the magical, unseen things are made of. And it's all much more visible at night—it glows in the dark, but only to people with the sight." I immediately think of glow sticks and glow-in-the-dark stickers, how they only show up in darkness. "Your eyes will take a while to adjust."

"The invisible fabric I read about in the guide, it's basically magic?" I ask, nodding to the strange and marvelous sights around us.

Ebb looks up, unimpressed, the same way I would look at an airplane or a car driving by.

"Yeah. Like me, all this has always been there. You just haven't noticed."

Then, as simple as that, he turns back toward the cliffs and we follow him—down the rambling dirt path that leads along the grassy clifftops toward the woods. I've walked this path before, but never at night. And I have no idea of how far we're going, or where. Luckily, the moon lights our way.

After a few minutes of silence, Ebb seems to take pity on us, because he hangs back a little. "Of course, ghosts are the flimsiest of all, the least powerful, the fabric spread *thin*, I guess." He clears his throat. "Witches, like you read, are made of much sturdier stuff—as are their familiars. They are part magic, part real, like the book says, though still invisible to most humans."

As we walk, we catch sight of the occasional ghost drifting along the path or through the nearby trees. Most turn to look at us, and then, seeming to dislike being seen in return, hurry away.

"I didn't know our woods were so haunted," I say.

"Oh, this is nothing. Every place in the world is haunted. Living people completely miss the whole thing.

Makes them feel quite alone, the things they don't see."
And then he adds, pensively, "I was surprised too—when I
died and saw it all. You get used to it."

Ebb floats on down the path, and we follow, getting
farther and farther away from home. Once or twice I see
him do something puzzling—reach down to his shirt
pocket, open it, and whisper to it. Is it possible for a person
to be dead and also delusional?

"I thought ghosts were supposed to be scary," Germ
whispers to me as we walk. "But this one just seems kind
of . . . moody. And I still don't know why I have the
sight."

I speak up, so Ebb can hear. "You said *people like me,
from families like mine* have a strong connection to the
unseen things. Is Germ from a family of witch hunters
too?" Germ's mom seems even *less* likely to be a witch
hunter than mine. She bakes cookies. She wears sweat-
shirts that say *I Could Be Wrong but Probably Not*. She
watches home decorating shows.

Ebb looks over at Germ, perplexed, and shakes his
head.

"I have no idea why Germ can see it all too. I never
heard anything about her or her family having the sight."

I'm starting to lose my bearings, and Germ and I have to step around or over bushes and brambles that Ebb floats right through—so we are soon out of breath, our arms and legs scratched up. Then we crest a small hill, and what's on the other side comes into view. Germ stumbles in fright as I let out a small cry.

There must be fifty ghosts gathered in the hollow below us, so many luminous spirits in one place that the whole field is aglow—some dressed as sailors in rain slickers, some in handspun clothes, others in finery. They're scattered among a hodgepodge maze of crooked, crumbling headstones, and they're all looking at us—but it's clear from the very first moment: they're not happy to see us.

Hovering in front of us, Ebb gestures for us not to move.

SEAPORT HISTORIC CEMETERY, a sign says, just within my view at the edge of the field. ESTABLISHED 1782. DEDICATED TO THE PEACEFUL REPOSE OF OUR TOWN'S SOULS.

A ghost floats up the hill toward us. He's mean-looking—one arm lopped off below the shoulder and bound with a rag, the other covered in tattoos of giant squids, mermaids, dragons, and anchors. His face is horribly scarred, copper-colored skin gone bluish and bright, one eye sagging.

I realize suddenly, Ebb is not our friend. He's led us here, away from witches, to a cemetery full of angry ghosts instead. He is a vengeful ghost leading us to our deaths.

The man floats closer, and I notice that worms can be ghosts too when I see a translucent one squiggling out of his ear. He leans down to look into my eyes with his one good one. Then he looks at Ebb, straightening up.

"There's word a witch is about in these parts tonight," he says to Ebb. "I hope you don't bring trouble here."

Ebb shifts nervously, floating back and then forward an inch.

"This is Rosie Oaks," he says. "Annabelle Oaks's daughter. Rosie, this is Homer."

The man stares at me another long minute, this time in surprise. His face softens, and his anger is replaced by recognition. And then concern.

"And I'm afraid we do bring trouble," Ebb adds nervously. "We've got a problem." He gives me a sort of encouraging look. Maybe he's not leading us to our deaths after all.

"The Memory Thief has found out about her?" Homer

says heavily, as if a weight of worry has just landed on his shoulders.

Ebb nods. He recounts the events of the night quickly, looking down at his feet sheepishly. When he gets to the part about Germ charging the moths, Germ flushes bright red and starts looking down at her feet too.

Homer stands for a long time, taking it in. Then he turns to me.

"Your life has changed forever, Rosie Oaks. You've gotten the sight, and I'm afraid you can't go back now to unseeing. And now you have found out that the world is both better and worse than you thought." He looks around at the other ghosts, up at the sky, still moving with its strange cloudlike figures and pink light. "I'm sorry about it. But now we have to figure out how to keep you alive." He mutters something under his breath at the moon. And then he sighs. "Come with me," he says.

CHAPTER 9

We stumble our way across the cemetery. The ground is sunken over graves in places and makes a sickening squish beneath us. I trip into a headstone, which elicits a cry from one of the ghosts.

"Respect my grave!" he yells across the hollow.

"We're sorry!" Germ mumbles, her face flushing.

The ghosts don't part for us, even though we keep saying, "Excuse me, excuse me."

"Forgive their manners," Homer says nervously, scanning the woods as if expecting danger at any moment.

"Most of them haven't been noticed by a living person since they died. Just walk right through them."

After hesitating for a moment, I step through a ghost blocking my way. Then another. Then another. Germ does the same. It gives me an icky, unsettling feeling, and Germ looks slightly nauseated.

"I know they're a gloomy lot," Homer says with an apologetic look. "You would be too, though, I guess, if all you wanted was to move *Beyond,* to the *up there*"—he casts his eyes to the pink hazy ring of the sky—"but you were stuck here."

"Why can't they just go up there?" I ask. "Just float up to the sky?"

"We can't fly, for one thing." Homer looks at me, his urgent expression softening into a smile. "And anyway, we are *tied*: earth-tied, home-tied. We have our haunts—our graves, the place where we lived, the place where we died, perhaps a place or two that has special significance to us. But trying to leave those places *thins* us, drains us."

I look up at the pink hazy sky.

"Why would you want to go up there anyway?" I ask. It does look beautiful, but also mysterious, strange, unknowable.

Homer comes to a stop for a moment, considering.

"Why *there*, my dear, is moving on. It's where we're all meant to go. Eventually. And until then, we wait. Some ghosts get to move on right away." He nods to the sky again. "And others don't. A lot of us just can't let the past go, and some of us—I think—have unfinished business of some sort. Something we need to wrap up, or fix, before we depart this earth. That's my theory anyway. Nobody ever tells us."

"What's *your* unfinished business?" Germ asks.

Homer shrugs. "Me? Could be to avenge myself against the squid who drowned me," he says pensively, "but I just don't know. I wish I did. It's dreadful to be *stuck*." He casts another glance around at the woods, then moves on.

At the far end of the hollow is an enormous crypt, and we make our way in that direction as Homer chatters on—clearly on edge, but also kind. He has a gentle, thoughtful air about him as he talks. Already, I like him much more than I like Ebb, who toggles from melancholy, to friendly, to angry and annoyed so fast that I can't make him out. Right now he's kicking at stones sullenly, his foot passing through them.

"Still," Homer continues, "once you die and become a ghost, you start believing the impossible . . . because you yourself are impossible. And that's comforting in its way."

He points to a tattoo on his biceps, the one of the giant squid. "Got this long before I died. Kind of ironic, considering what killed me, but still glad I have it. Reminds me to always stay present. I found out about meditating after I died. Helps a lot. Ghosts aren't usually good at *being present*, considering we are actually shadows of the past." He looks around, bemused.

"I cope with it all by staying nosy. I know way too much about every living and dead person within five miles of Seaport, plus local history, all the sports teams within fifty miles, and of course, you and your mom." He points to his head. "I'm a stickler for gossip, is what it boils down to. That's why Ebb's brought you to me. I know all about your mom. Then again, *everybody* knows *something* about your mom. And now we all know what kind of danger you're in."

We've come to a stop at the edge of the crypt, which has the words "Homer Honeycutt, captain of the *Mary Sue*. Sunken on the rocks of Cape Horn and devoured by a squid, 1886."

"Well, this is home, such as it is."

Homer gestures for us to sit on a low stone ledge of the crypt. We perch awkwardly, Germ swinging her legs like she does when she's sitting on bleachers at a football game.

"Respect our graves!" a ghost yells at us from behind, making us jump, and Germ's legs go still.

"So," Homer says, folding his hands, an ominous worry settling over his luminous features, "the Memory Thief has found you. And now if you're to escape her, you need to know some things. Things that have been hidden from you, just as you yourself have been hidden."

Homer is about to go on when a ghost lets out a moan, and Homer shoots him a look and shakes his head.

"So far in your life, you've learned only the history of the seen and the living. Now, if you are to survive, you need the history of the living *and* the dead, the seen *and* the unseen."

Beside me, Germ shivers—possibly with fear, possibly with excitement. I cross my arms over my chest. If there's one thing I know how to do, it's to be quiet and listen.

Homer lowers his head, as if thinking about where to begin. To our surprise, he starts with the moon.

"At the beginning of time," Homer begins, eyeing us sharply, with urgency, "there were the thirteen witches and there was the Moon Goddess, all made of magic. The Moon Goddess, hidden and mysterious—who herself created our moon and many others—gathers up light and sends it down at night as a dim glow onto earth's darkness, bringing strange powers with it: hope, dreams, imagination . . . mysterious things we don't fully know or understand. The witches, on the other hand, are made of all the ugliness you can imagine. You simply can't have a thing without having its opposite, and the Moon Goddess is so powerful, it took thirteen witches to balance out her worth.

"The goddess and the witches have been at war, always. But they fight each other in different ways. The Moon Goddess is subtle, and I guess unfathomable. She stays far away, and doesn't meddle directly in earthly things. The witches, on the other hand, are not subtle at all. Their desire is to sow chaos, unhappiness, and discord among humans. War, despair, loss, grief, anguish . . . their fingerprints are on all of it. And they love it; chaos is to a witch what water is to a fish."

Homer pauses. "Now, all living creatures die, the world churns. Darkness and light, you see, are part of nature, and neither can ever fully leave us. But the witches are always trying to tip the scales in their favor."

His brow furrows as he goes on. "In the last hundred years or so, it seems they've been succeeding. They've sown more discord upon the earth than ever before."

Ebb, who has been hovering at the edge of the crypt, looks at me sorrowfully. Homer falls into silence, wincing as if what he's about to tell me will be the hardest part of all. And then, instead, the corner of his mouth lifts into a kind smile.

"But there's hope, merely because there are people who've fought back. And this brings us to your family." He looks at me for a long time, and my arms begin to swim with chills.

"The women in your family have all had the gift of sight. People call it ESP, or being psychic, or whatever else. Mostly living people are"—he shrugs in a defeated kind of way—"oblivious to the unseen things all around them. A few are more aware, but they use their abilities for small things: telling fortunes, finding missing socks, stuff like that."

Germ nods sagely beside me and interjects, "Reading pets' minds."

Homer blinks at her for a second, then looks at me. "*Your* family has used it differently," Homer continues. "You are the last in a long line of women who used their seeing abilities—abilities they could have used to find socks, or read fortunes, or read pets' minds, I suppose—to seek out witches and how to hunt them."

"Like, with swords and stuff?" Germ asks.

Homer shakes his head. "Witches can't be wounded by any mortal method. Lunging at a witch with a sword is like fighting air. But the women in your family, they *have* invented their *own* weapons, capable of hurting witches—and killing them—though to our knowledge that only happened *once*, in Sweden in 1612, when your way-back-quintuple-great-grandmother killed a witch called the Trapper."

He shakes his head again as if trying to shake the image out of his mind.

"Since then, no one has managed it." He pauses. "Because, well . . . the witches can no longer be found."

"Can't be found?" I echo.

Homer tilts his head to look at us solemnly.

"Witches, as powerful as they are, are cowardly creatures. After that first killing, they disappeared somewhere beyond this world—nobody knows where, or how. They only return once a month at the dark moon, when the moonlight can't find or burn them, to lay their curses, before fading back to wherever they hide. The few witch hunters on earth haven't even had a fighting chance of killing witches because they haven't been able to track them down. One by one, *they've* been found instead, and cursed."

Homer looks out over the horizon at the sea. A shadow creeps across the crypt as a cloud crosses over the moon.

"But the Memory Thief . . . ," I say.

"It's rumored that the Memory Thief is an exception—that somehow, while the others hide far away, she was left behind to lurk on earth for some reason we don't know."

"Still, there's one strong, brave, *exceptional* person who we've come to suspect *did* find the witches, who discovered the great secret of how to reach them where they hide, and destroy them. Not just the Memory Thief, but all of them." He turns to look at me. "The problem is, of course, that she's forgotten."

I have a prickly feeling. A sea-urchin-in-my-chest feeling.

"That person, Rosie, was your mother."

CHAPTER 10

An old ache, a buried hurt, rises up beside my confusion.

My mom is not strong or brave. She doesn't even like to walk down the driveway to get the mail. She doesn't even make toast. She doesn't even know how to love me. And yet she has figured out the key to fighting the greatest forces of darkness in the universe?

I feel all the things I've missed piling on me at once. Birthdays she could have cared about, nights when we could have read together, hugs and inside jokes. I think of the mom who painted my room, the one who painted, *Look at how a single candle can both defy and define the darkness.* Was she once really all the things Homer says she was? I want to believe it and I'm scared to believe it.

Germ lays a hand on my arm. Homer sighs, looking at me with pity, which angers me. I'm angry and sad and hopeful at once.

A breeze blows cold across us.

"All of this brings us to you," Homer says. "And how you yourself are an impossible thing."

I hesitate. "Impossible how?"

"Well"—he pauses, looking around the cemetery and up at the sky, as if gauging the time he has to answer—"the stories of you both are woven mostly of rumors and gossip. We ghosts have quite a network—ghosts meeting up in fields, at cemeteries, out on the sea, passing along information. I can only tell you what I know. But I'll have to do it quickly.

"I know that your mother left home at sixteen to travel the world searching for witches, and preserved everything she learned in *The Witch Hunter's Guide to the Universe.* And that *her* mother—your grandmother—had passed along the book to her just before being cursed by Mable the Mad and wandering off into the woods, never to be seen again." He eyes me for my reaction as I listen breath-lessly. *My grandmother, cursed, lost.*

"I know that somewhere in your mother's travels, while crossing the sea by freighter on one of her journeys, she met your father. I know that she showed up here in Sea-port after he died, with just a suitcase and a growing belly and a key to the house on Waterside Road."

My skin prickles at the mention of my father, but Homer pushes on quickly, before I can ask more.

"It didn't take the ghosts who haunt your house long to figure out who she was—we ghosts have known about the Oakses for years. And it didn't take long for us to see she was hiding, and to guess whom she was *hiding from*." For a moment pity overtakes him, deepening the lines on his face. "The ghosts at your house, including Ebb, watched her stash *The Witch Hunter's Guide* under the floor and wait for your arrival. She was hiding your history from you, I suppose. She was already, before you were born, hiding your sight. She was turning her back on all of it."

"But why?" I finally interrupt.

Homer looks at me sadly. "As I think Ebb has told you, those with the sight stand out in the world like a beacon, easy for witches to find. Most of them pose no threat to witches. And a witch hunter can learn to sort of . . . *dim* themselves, a mental trick that's hard to master. But the daughter of a witch hunter, a defenseless child . . . well, I suspect that, despite all her courage, she couldn't face the possibility of losing you."

I swallow the lump in my throat.

"And she might have had a chance to live a normal life with you. Only . . ."

"Only?"

Homer wrings his hands together and lowers his voice, looking around the cemetery again as if keeping an eye out for the Memory Thief herself.

"Only, somewhere in her travels—we believe—she'd discovered the enormous secret of finding and reaching the witches. The rumors circulated quite a bit at the time. And those rumors, I believe, made it to the witches' ears." He leans back, as if he doesn't want to say what he has to say next. "And even though the famous Annabelle Oaks had given up hunting witches, a witch came for her any-way. And for you. And that's the impossible thing."

"What?" I ask, confused.

"Why, isn't it obvious?" he says. "You're still here."

Homer drops his voice lower still. He leans toward us, and speaks so quietly, we have to lean forward to hear him.

"The night you were born, your mother was cursed. That much is obvious. When she went to the hospital to have you, she was the same powerful woman we had always heard about. But when she came out, her memories were gone; she was just a shell of a person.

"As the newborn daughter of the woman who had so threatened the witches and their secrets, the Memory Thief should have hated you, even feared you. And you were but a helpless baby; it would have been so easy for her to curse you, too, or to bid her familiars to steal you. But for some reason that we can't begin to guess, you weren't taken. Your mother's *memories* were—but not you." He smiles gently.

"Your mother somehow saved you, Rosie. We don't know how. In my heart, un-beating as it is, I believe that means something—a powerful secret. There's no other way to explain it. But no one can imagine what it might be."

"The Memory Thief," I offer, "she said something about being tricked."

Homer contemplates this, then shakes his head. "I don't know. I've spoken to every ghost who haunts that hospital, and none of them can tell me anything useful. They all fled when they sensed a witch in the vicinity that night, and never looked back. It's a dead end, no pun intended."

He gazes at me, then leans back, swipes a worm gently out of his ear and drops it onto the ground. He looks at us. He thinks for a long time.

"All I know is that the Memory Thief is coming for you *now*. And to *stay* safe, you'll have to go far from here. Give up everything you know. Go into hiding."

"For how long?" Germ asks for me.

He blinks at me a moment, taken aback. "Why, forever."

He does not seem to notice that he has shocked us. He looks down at his hands as if counting on his fingers, working out logistics under his breath. "There are people who could hide you, take you in, all over the world—in Japan, in Zimbabwe . . . a few brave people with the sight, scattered remnants of witch hunting families who'd take the risk for one of their own. All that matters is that you're safe and away from here come the dark moon."

"What about Germ? Is she in danger too?"

He looks at Germ, then shakes his head. "She's got the sight for some reason I can't guess. I suppose it *could* be a coincidence. But she's not a witch hunter. As long as she stays uninvolved, they'll ignore her. It's you the witch wants. And she'll be angry. A witch can't kill, directly. But her familiars are something to be reckoned with, and there are many ways a witch's curse can cause you to end up dead—to wander off a cliff, say, or jump from the deck of a ship."

I'm afraid—so afraid that my heart feels like it has fallen into my feet—but an entirely different idea now catches hold of me. And I know, now that it's caught, it won't un-catch. I don't say it at first.

"My mom would never come with me," I say instead. "She won't leave sight of the sea." I think of how agitated she gets when we're away from the shore for just a couple of hours.

And then I find the courage to ask what I most want to know. It causes that same prickling, heavy, sea-urchin-in-the-chest feeling that I've felt all night. And now I realize what it is. The painful, lopsided, unfamiliar feeling that has been rising in me for hours is a scary, risky, prickly kind of hope.

"Um, Homer, you talk about all these curses that witches cast by touching someone. Can a curse be broken?"

Homer blinks at me and leans back, his brow furrowing in concern.

"Rosie . . ."

He hesitates for a long time before he finally speaks again.

"I don't know everything about witches, but I do know that the only way to kill a curse is to kill the witch who wields it. And only one person, by some fluke we can't begin to guess at, has ever killed a witch. Even an adult twice your size would not be able to do it. Even a trained soldier. Even your mom couldn't."

"But if I could get my hands on a witch weapon like the kind you were talking about—"

"It's not so easy to do that, I'm afraid. The witch hunters have secrets just like the witches do—and the biggest one is their weapons. We don't know how they made them, or where any of them are. I doubt even the guide will give you much help there."

"But . . . ," I say, and can't find the words. I think of how Germ's mom says the day Germ was born was like getting the deed to a Hawaiian island. If I broke the curse, would my mom feel that way about me? Would she look at me like Mrs. Bartley looks at Germ? The thought makes me dizzy.

An itchy, watched feeling makes me turn to Ebb. He's staring at me intently with a strange look on his face—sorry and guilty and uncertain all at once. But before I can try to make sense of the look, Homer speaks again. "Rosie, once, your mother loved you with all her heart, and that counts for something, even if she's forgotten it now. And her only wish was that you be safe. She would have never wanted you to be a witch hunter."

"I don't want to hunt *witches*. I just want to hunt *one* witch. I could just stay and kill the one witch."

"You can't stay. It's out of the question."

Beside me, I feel Germ studying me. She clearly wants me to run, like everyone else, but she also knows me better than anyone else. People assume that because I'm small and quiet, I'm also easy to go along with things. I am not. Germ shakes her head.

"Rosie won't go," she says.

Homer stares at us a moment, then scans the woods around the cemetery, nervous.

"We ghosts couldn't help you, you know—we ghosts— if you got in trouble." He looks at Ebb, who's been listening quietly in the background. "We're only shadows, remnants—our uselessness is our greatest burden. Even if we could fight, which we can't, the fate of a ghost who crosses a witch is worse than death. If you stay, if—and *when*—she comes for you, we can't save you. You'd be completely on your own."

I sit very still. My stomach hurts. It feels like I've swallowed a bag full of rocks. But Germ has always said I've had a piece of iron lodged in my back that won't budge once I decide something.

I can't leave my mom. Especially when I know there's a tiny, tiny sliver of a chance I could . . . fix her.

Homer sighs, relenting, but exasperated.

"If you want to kill the Memory Thief, Rosie, you'd have to do two things: find a witch weapon or how to make one, and find out how your mom saved you the night you were born—why and how you were never taken. But let's be clear: I'm against it."

He sounds bitterly worried and disappointed as he continues, "Remember, at the dark moon, she'll be back for you. There's no getting around it."

I knead my hands together, too filled with worry to reply. And seeing this, Homer seems to take pity on me. He slumps a little, and smiles at me.

"Take heart, Rosie," he says. "Only the witches would have you think there is more darkness in the world than there is light. Only they would have you believe that love could ever really leave you."

He ruminates for a moment, then stiffens. "The moon is low. You'd better go so Ebb can get you home before he disappears at dawn, like we all do. I've kept you too long."

I stand on unsteady legs and glance at Ebb, who still has the guilty, uncertain look on his face.

"I'd shake your hand," Homer says, "but you'll just have to settle for me saying it's an honor to meet one of the famous Oaks women at long last. And I hope our paths cross again."

Germ tugs my sleeve. Ebb is already making his way across the cemetery, impatient now, and we turn to follow him.

Looking over my shoulder, I see Homer waving as we hurry away, until he is hidden beyond the trees.

CHAPTER 11

"I like him," Germ says wistfully. "He's moody but he's kind of cute."

We're rambling back along the uneven cliff-side trail toward home, and I realize, after puzzling over it for a minute, that Germ is talking about Ebb—who leads the way, his head hanging low. This makes it official that Germ thinks every boy on earth is cute, even dead ones. And also that Germ can face anything in the world, even the news of a magical unseen layer underneath all existence, and still stride through life like usual.

"Though, I guess he'll be thirteen forever," Germ muses. "Then again, we'll catch up to him in a couple of years," she says brightly. "Then again," she says flatly, "we'll get older than him really fast."

Up ahead, Ebb is gloomy, lost in thought. And then he pivots suddenly toward us.

"You should run, Rosie, like Homer says. I don't think you understand what you're up against. You only just learned about all this stuff and you have no idea how terrifying it can get. Even if you had a weapon . . . ," he says, and gets lost in a thought for a moment, then refocuses, shaking his head. "I can't help you when she comes. We ghosts are useless, like Homer said. We can't affect *anything*, really. And if we tangle with witches—" He stops himself.

"What?"

Ebb doesn't answer. He looks down at the ground, thinking. All the while, he seems to be patting something in his pocket, checking on it occasionally.

"Maybe we can get someone *living* to help us," Germ says. "Like someone . . . adult."

I nod in agreement. "And I can show my mom the book she hid. Maybe things could come back to her if she sees what she wrote with her own hands."

Ebb looks unconvinced. "Trust me, none of it will

work. Nobody will believe you. And your mom won't understand. That piece of her is gone."

"Ebb," Germ ventures, as if she's going to say something profound. "You can be kind of a downer," she blurts out instead. "I'm just being honest."

Ebb brightens and fades momentarily. I suppose it's the ghost version of a blush. Then he goes blank, like he's given up. He pulls whatever it is out of his pocket, cupping it gently in his hand—and I finally see what it is. A spider. Or at least, a ghost of one. Germ and I exchange a look.

"Is that your . . . little friend?" Germ asks softly, casting me a look.

Ebb glances back at us. "We died on the same day," he says curtly. He replaces the spider in his pocket and floats on in silence.

"And it talks?" Germ asks, never one to pick up on subtle social cues, like when people don't want to discuss something.

"*All* of nature talks in its own way," he says, but won't elaborate further. Germ looks at me like she's not so sure that Ebb isn't crazy.

As we linger for a moment, I look to the horizon for any sign of the memory moths returning or a witch approaching (though, I'm not sure exactly how witches approach places—on brooms?), despite Homer's reassurances about witches steering clear of moonlight. Dread sits heavy in the pit of my stomach.

But then, something else in the sky takes my breath—not a witch, but something even more stunning and strange.

I don't know how I could have missed seeing it. It lies low over a cliff that juts out into the ocean: the bright crescent moon and something—a *ladder*, as impossible as that is—dangles down from its edge, just grazing the clifftops.

Ebb and Germ both follow my gaze.

"What is that?" I ask, nodding toward it.

Ebb is quiet for a moment. "It's an invitation, to any brave enough to accept," he finally says.

"Invitation to what?"

He shoots a look at me as if I've asked a really obvious question. "To the moon."

I think back to what Homer was saying about the Moon Goddess. It's hard, in a way, to believe she really exists. But the ladder makes it suddenly real. I think for a moment about astronauts, landing on the moon and not knowing there's an invisible Moon Goddess hovering around them.

My heart leaps.

"Why don't we just climb the ladder? We could ask her what we should do about the Memory Thief. She could help us!"

I feel sudden hope flooding over me, but Ebb is shaking his head.

"It's probably been centuries since anyone's climbed up there," he says. "You can only climb it if the Moon Goddess allows it. Otherwise, when you get about halfway up, the ladder disappears and . . ." He whistles and makes a plunging motion with his hand. "Nobody ever really tries it."

My spirits drop. "That's terrible. I thought she was supposed to be good."

Ebb flickers as he thinks how to explain. "The Moon Goddess *is* a force of good, but she keeps her own plans, and she's very exacting, and I suppose only the purehearted and brave can make it all the way to her. Otherwise the witches would probably climb up." His shoulders droop with gloom. "Anyway, she wants people to help themselves; she can't fight their battles for them. At least, that's what all the legends say."

I look up at the moon, anger prickling. What's the

point of being a good and wise Moon Goddess if you don't *help*? But Germ's mind is on another tack.

"Ghosts have legends?" she asks.

"Sure," Ebb says. "Like that beyond that pink haze is a paradise for all the souls who've moved on. And like the sea contains all the time that's ever existed and you can travel through it in the mouth of a magical whale."

"Is that true?" I ask.

Ebb considers for a moment, then shakes his head slowly. "It's just wishful thinking."

"Wishful why?"

Ebb shrugs.

"Ghosts and time. It's the thing that torments us. Too much of it now that we are dead, too little of it when we weren't." He smiles ruefully. "The Time Witch has a lot to answer for with us."

I remember skimming past the Time Witch in *The Witch Hunter's Guide*, a woman with clocks dangling from her neck. But the Memory Thief is the only witch I can think about.

We stand gazing at the setting moon—which glows, aloof and distant, above the mirror of the sea for a few more moments before it sinks out of sight. I think of my mom and dad, meeting somewhere out at sea so long ago—somewhere in the time when the ghosts lost track of her, before she showed up in Seaport with me in her tummy. And then a spark ignites inside me.

I turn to Ebb, try to grab his arm, but my fingers, of course, slip through him instead.

"My mom likes to say, 'He's out there swimming, waiting for me.' I used to think she was talking about my dad. Do you think he could be a ghost, out there somewhere, swimming? Do you think she's talking about him?"

Ebb looks at me for a moment. He glances sadly up to the glowing haze above.

"I'm sorry, Rosie. I've heard nothing about your dad except what Homer said, that your mom met him on a freighter while crossing the ocean back when she was chasing witches." He squints as if trying to remember. "And that he drowned before you were born. Not because of witch mischief or anything like that, I don't think. Just because . . . bad things happen."

Unanswerable questions rise up one after the other about my dad—*What was he like? Did he have the sight too? Did he love my mom from the moment he met her?* I feel an empty place inside ache. Ebb waits for me to say something, but I'm silent, so he continues.

"The ghosts who stay behind are a rarity, Rosie. Most times people are just *gone*, Beyond. Your dad—if he were out there somewhere, I think we would have heard about it by now."

I stare down at my feet, crestfallen. But why would my mom always talk about someone waiting for her in the sea, if it's not him? I tuck and fold the hope inside me to think about later in secret. Maybe that feeling of always missing another half—maybe that's my heart knowing my dad is somewhere out there, trying to find me and help me.

There's a deep kindness in Ebb's voice when he speaks again.

"I know it's not the same as having a mom and dad who are really there for you, but you were never alone, Rosie, even though you felt like you were. The times you've woken up from nightmares and your mom wouldn't comfort you. The times you've fallen and she didn't get you a Band-Aid. Your first steps that she ignored. I've been here through all of it; all of us ghosts in your house have. You just couldn't see it."

I stare at him quietly, feeling my face flush. Even though he's trying to be nice, I don't like the idea of ghosts lingering around for my whole life without me knowing it—not at all. I've always been a secretive kind of person—especially about my feelings. I like to keep myself a secret from pretty much everyone but Germ. And now I wonder, how many of my secrets does Ebb know?

The night is just beginning to fade when we see the warm lights of my house up ahead, glowing through the dark wet dimness. Several ghosts are floating across the lawn as if leaving after a long night's haunt.

A small creature, all fangs and claws, is running across the grass toward us, and he lunges at my leg, though he passes right through it. He growls and snarls up at me before lurching away.

"What was that?" I ask, shuddering. *An evil creature?* I wonder. *A witch's familiar?*

"Just the ghost of a rabid possum," Ebb says. "He's a mean old thing, tries to bite everybody. We all wish he'd move on, honestly."

We are just venturing onto the grass when I almost walk right into a flesh-and-blood, breathing man.

I stumble back, shocked. It takes a few moments of staring and getting my bearings to realize it's only Gerald, the guy who sometimes fixes things around the property, whom I pay with my mom's checkbook.

Germ and I stand frozen in our tracks, Ebb hovering between us. We stare at Gerald and Gerald stares back. And then he smiles.

"You two are up early," he says. Neither Germ nor I can find words to reply, because we are waiting for him to notice Ebb.

"Um," I say, "we were . . . bird-watching."

Gerald cocks his head at me. "Birds?"

"You have to get up early to see the red-breasted, uh, warble . . . um . . . jay," Germ puts in.

Gerald stares at us for a moment, then nods. At the same time, a translucent old woman—the washerwoman I saw last night—barrels through him with an arm full of filmy sheets, and Germ almost loses it, snorting into her hand.

"Bless you," I say.

"Well, no rest for the weary," Gerald says, after giving us another strange look. He then walks across the lawn to his truck to get his supplies, as the last of the ghosts but Ebb trickle into the woods beyond him. We let out the breaths we've been holding.

"Well," Germ says, eyeing Gerald but turning to me. She has circles under her eyes. "I better get home. My mom wanted me there by seven. And maybe she *will* believe me, about everything. Maybe she can help."

I look at her, feeling guilty suddenly—all the night's seemingly impossible events catching up to me.

"Germ," I say, "I don't know how you can *see*. But the witches . . . all of this is my problem. I don't want you to be in danger too."

"It's *our* problem," Germ says. "I feel like I caught the sight from you somehow, and I'm happy I did." She frowns. "But, Rosie, I want you to be safe. I think you should really think about running like Ebb and Homer say."

"I'll think about it," I say slowly, looking to Ebb, who watches us silently. It hurts a little, because I can't imagine ever leaving Germ, and I wonder how she can encourage me to leave.

She gives me a quick wave and gets on one of the rusty old bikes that we share, by the shed. As soon as she's gone, things feel emptier and scarier.

"Well, I'll be back tonight," Ebb says.

I turn to him. "From now on, maybe you could give me some privacy," I say. "I really appreciate all your help, but would you mind just . . . staying outside the house from now on? I mean, you're a boy, for one thing. It's sort of . . ."

Ebb's mouth drops closed, then straightens into a thin,

embarrassed line. His glow dims a little. He nods. Then he turns and drifts across the grass without another word. A moment later, as the sun rises above the lip of the sea, he vanishes completely.

Inside, I climb the stairs and look in on my mom, who's asleep.

She is peaceful in her bed, despite the wild night that's passed.

When she wakes, I'll show her the book and see if she can remember. But in my heart of hearts, I think that she'll wake and look at me with foggy eyes and try her hardest to remember things, and fail, like she always does. She'll go about her day as if I'm not here. She'll sit and look out at the sea.

For now I crawl into bed and hope for a couple of hours' sleep. I tap out on my fingers the four days till the dark moon. I have so much to find out before then. What secret saved me the night I was born? Is it the same secret my mom found out about fighting witches? What weapon can I use to defend myself?

I pull *The Witch Hunter's Guide* into bed with me and flip slowly through the pages until I reach the section called "The Oakses and Their Weapons."

As Homer warned, it's a disappointment. There is only

one simple paragraph about weapons, at the very beginning of the section. It reads: *A weapon is as much a part of a witch hunter as her fingernails or her teeth. It is tied right to her heart, and that's where she keeps it close. The secret of it is passed on from mother to daughter, a gift of magic and material combined: an embroidered dress for a shield, a sword made of song, a net knit from poetry.*

It doesn't make sense. How does anyone knit a net of poetry, or embroider a shield? It sounds simple and impossible at the same time. And one thing is for sure, my mother never passed on the secret to me.

Beyond this, there are old photos pasted onto the pages, from as far back as the days of blurry old black-and-whites of ladies in long dresses with bustles. My family—all the women. People I have never heard of, but whom I long for. A woman with a severe gray bun, *Dorothy Oaks, cursed with madness*—my grandmother? A woman with scraggly brown hair, holding a fine leather-bound dagger, *Mary Lee Oaks, struck with babble and confusion*. A woman in a beautiful dress stitched all over with pictures, *Eugenia Oaks, cursed to forget*. And my heart sinks seeing them, as I read the curses by their names.

Women who knew more than me, who never had their sight hidden from them, who grew up learning to fight, and were told the secrets of their family tree. They *all* met terrible ends. They were blotted out. Every single one.

Who am I—a girl who didn't know even about the invisible fabric until this night—to think I can do what they couldn't?

I look out the window, thinking about the Memory Thief. How she blotted my mom out—taking all the love out of her, and with it, all the fight. She is going to blot me out too, in four days, if I can't figure out how to kill her first.

Maybe I should run.

But then I think again about my mom. I wonder if maybe the love Homer says she felt for me could be hidden inside her like a muscle memory, like the way a person plays the piano without thinking about it. Like if once she got a little of it, it would all come back to her.

And then it lands on me—the sudden, breathless, horribly hurtful hope. To have someone look at me like I'm a light their eyes are drawn to. To have a real mom, which would mean a real family, which would mean I, myself, am a real, lovable daughter.

If that's not worth risking your life for, I don't know what is.

PART 2

CHAPTER 12

I wake in the late morning with Homer Honeycutt's words in my head: *Find a witch weapon or how to make one, and find out how your mom saved you the night you were born.*

I know the first place I need to start, but it doesn't fill me with much hope. I need to start with *her*.

Bleary-eyed from so little sleep, I tuck the *Guide* under my arm and head downstairs to make myself my first-ever cup of coffee. It's bitter and I don't like the taste, but it wakes me up. *You're gonna stunt your growth, sweetie,* I think.

I make my mom a cup and bring it to her in the attic, where she already sits, rocking and staring out the window.

She looks up at me and narrows her eyes. I glance around at all the things I've put up to help her remember me. I kneel beside her with the book. I slide *The Witch Hunter's Guide to the Universe* onto her lap.

Her eyes go from her coffee cup to the book, then to me. There is something there. A glimmer of a spark of memory.

"Mom, do you remember this book? It's a book you helped to write," I say, "full of secrets you helped to learn."

She blinks at me, then stares back down at the cover. I slowly open it for her, and flip through one page and then the next, my heart beating in my throat with hope. When I arrive at the page of the Memory Thief, her eyelids flutter. She turns her gaze to the window.

I look hard at her. "Mom," I say, low, because my voice falters. "What happened the night I was born? How did you protect me? What secrets did you know?"

She turns her eyes back to me. And that's when I see it, or I think I do. Somewhere deep inside her eyes, something trying to get out, to reach me. Maybe I'm imagining it, but I don't think so; it's like the smallest pinprick of light still inside her. And then it fades.

"What are you asking me?" she says. "What is this? Why are you bothering me?"

I squeeze her hand tight. *What did you expect?* I think.

"I'm not giving up," I say. "I'm going to find you—the old you. I'm going to rescue you from the monster in the fairy tale. I'm going to bring you back."

She blinks at the book. She shakes her head a few times as if clearing it of a dream. "That would be nice, Rosie," she says, and then she looks away as if I've already left the room.

I close the book and pull it onto my lap, fingering the edges, knowing that any help my mom could offer is not worth hoping for. I know she'll sit all day staring at the sea, forgetting me, the book, everything, like a ghost herself. I'm on my own.

I call Germ and leave her a message, just checking in. And then I set my mind to the first thing I need to do. Booby traps.

There's an old movie Germ left here once called *Home Alone*, about a boy who has to protect his house from thieves, and I rewatch it to see how he lays traps for the bad guys, taking notes in one of my school binders. Homer said no human weapon can hurt a witch—I haven't forgotten that. But even *he* said he didn't know everything about witches.

Based on what I learn, I get a shovel and a twenty-pound dumbbell I find in the attic. I turn broomsticks into spears; a jar of pennies, some soda cans, and some string into a homemade alarm system; and a box of nails into a gruesome paddleboard bat. There's an axe that hangs on the wall down in the basement, but I decide to steer clear of the basement altogether. I just don't have the courage to go down there now, even in daytime.

I break glasses in paper bags and place the bags by my window to use as bombs. Then I take a long tour through the fuse box and watch an online video about how to get wires to spark.

Once I'm finished with the traps, I turn to my mom's bedroom, not the one in the attic but the room that is *supposed* to be hers. Despite her general indifference to most things, it makes me nervous to sneak in without her knowing. So I try to do it as quietly and quickly as possible.

Coming in here has always felt like walking into a museum of the person my mom once was. There are old photos on the wall of her standing on a boat or in front of the Egyptian pyramids, holding a bow and arrow aloft proudly at summer camp with a blue ribbon on her chest, riding a horse, gazing at my dad with a joyful smile—a wild, brave, happy person. There is her diploma for art history. A soft purple bedspread lies over her queen bed; all sorts of stained-glass baubles hang in the window to turn sunlight into rainbows. There are paintings she once made of flowers and statues and people, things she painted while traveling the world. (Though, now I realize, with a deep chill, she was traveling the world *hunting witches*.) All her subjects have personalities: a rose looks self-confident; a building looks tired; a statue of a man in robes, glimpsed through a painted window, looks curious and kind.

There are empty spots on her shelves where her books used to be, empty spaces left where I've stolen her knickknacks—retreating to my room with treasures in my arms, trying to steal bits of my mom, I guess.

Mostly she has either not noticed what I've taken, or not cared, but a few books she has stolen back: *Where the Wild Things Are, Hansel and Gretel, Rapunzel*. I go to them now, flip through the pages—which are full of witches and monsters, faeries and magic. Does she keep taking these books back because the secret to finding and killing witches is hidden on their pages? A witch getting pushed into an oven, a monster being tamed when you stare into its eyes?

But if there are clues in these books about how to fight a witch, I can't find one. I doubt I could push a witch into an oven or tame one with my eyes.

As quietly as I can, I search the rest of the room. It's disheveled and disorganized. I find Mom's wedding ring in a ceramic mug next to a chewed piece of gum; I find Mom's bank card in a pile of receipts, and an engraved pendant with her birth date on the floor. I look through folders, boxes, plastic bags.

And then I find, amongst a pile of blank postcards from places she must have visited once, my birth certificate.

It reads:

> State of Maine Certificate of Birth
> Place of Birth: Saint Ignatius Hospital
> Date of Birth: September 1, 2010
> Name of Child: Oaks, Rose Kristen
> Sex: Female
> Weight: 6 lbs, 8 oz
> Hair: Brown
> Eyes: Brown

I've seen the sign for Saint Ignatius Hospital many times. It's just at the edge of town, in a patch of woods at the start of a long empty road through the trees, the sign rotting away so that now it only says SAINT IGNAT SPITA. I don't even know if the hospital is still open, but I do know it's been displaced by a new, shiny hospital downtown. The new one I know really well because every time Germ breaks a bone doing something daring, we go there.

I gaze at my birth certificate for a while, at the date, wishing I could read more into this simple piece of paper than a few meaningless facts. And then—just as I'm tucking it back amongst the postcards—I notice there *is* something. Because on the back of the certificate, in a loose scrawl that is still my mom's, only messier than usual—are these words:

> Swimming.
> Swimming.
> Swimming.
> Waiting.
> Where is he????
> Where they hide from me.

As I stare at the words, my body prickles with chills.

Questions rise one after the other. Who is "he"? Does "where they hide" mean the witches?

Swimming, and the night I was born, and how I was saved, and where the witches hide—the great secret my mom supposedly discovered. They're linked somehow; they have to be. But how?

Just as I move to put the birth certificate away, I hear my mom stirring in the attic, then creaking down the stairs. I hurry out right as she comes to the landing. She looks at me for a moment, as if suspicious, and then brushes past me into the room.

By the time I fix dinner, the day is dimming to dusk. My heart begins to thrum a little faster, to know the night is coming, and all the strange things it brings with it. I can barely eat, I'm so nervous. I try Germ again on the phone, but she doesn't answer.

After I eat, I turn to *The Witch Hunter's Guide* again. I fight off sleep as I flip through the chapters, glancing at the legends. (There are plenty about the Moon Goddess and her ladder, and just as Ebb said, one about a whale who can swim through time, and some about ancient ghosts who tried to mount a rebellion against the witch Hypocriffa and lost.) There's a long description of the moon and gravity that I decide to come back to later.

Under "The Invisible World and Its Beings," there's a disclaimer that there are plenty of magical beings left to be discovered, followed by a list with drawings and descriptions of the ones that are known. The Moon Goddess. Ghosts. Witches. Witch familiars. Cloud shepherds. Curious, I zero in on this last one.

Made of mist like the clouds they guide, the cloud shepherds watch the happenings of the world from above. They are rain keepers, snow spillers, wind blowers. They are restless observers. They climb high over towns, wrap themselves around forests, whip over the waves. They've seen dinosaurs thrive, Atlantis sink, and Pompeii fall under ashes. And all the while, they watch the world, and listen, and see all. With a bird's-eye view and a vast memory, they know almost everything about human affairs and have memories of each person on earth.

They will sometimes share their knowledge if only you can reach them, but they are extremely elusive—only touching earth in fog: grazing mountaintops, lying

over the water, and they will dissipate
and disappear when approached. Like the
Moon Goddess, they do not interfere.

I sit back. What I would give to find a cloud shepherd and talk to it. But I suppose the likelihood of catching a cloud is about as high as the likelihood of pinning down the edge of a rainbow.

My eyelids are heavy, and none of this is helping me to uncover the secrets of killing a witch. I lay the book down, then walk up to my room and watch out the window as the sun sets. As it does, the magical world comes into focus.

Up in the sky, the cloud shepherds—now that I know what they are—move about, changing shapes as they go. The phantom ships materialize on the horizon, and the moon rises at the lip of the sea, its ladder dangling.

A light fog drifts up from the ocean and across the lawn. And then the ghosts begin to arrive. They emerge from the wispy edges of the fog—there must be twenty or more, and I catch my breath as I watch them.

Five peel off toward the house: the knitting woman I saw last night in the parlor, and the washerwoman from this morning (the two appear to be friends). The starfish-covered sailor in the yellow rain slicker, the lady in white. And—I shiver—the Murderer. As if he feels my eyes on him, he looks up at where I stand, and I go still with fright. For a moment our eyes meet, and his bore into mine with hatred.

Then the group drifts below and out of sight, no doubt floating into the rooms below.

After watching for another minute, I'm just about to turn away from the view when I see Ebb. He's standing at the edge of the trees across the lawn, apparently obeying my request not to come into the house, which makes me feel a pang of regret. (I'd much rather have Ebb here than the Murderer.) He doesn't notice me, though. For some reason he appears to be whispering to a cluster of fireflies.

I don't realize I'm being watched until I hear a strange dripping sound. Someone is standing behind me.

"It's the tragic ones who linger the longest, ain't it, little one?"

My arms swim with gooseflesh at the raspy voice. I turn to see—not the Murderer but the starfish-covered sailor standing in the hallway, dripping luminous water that doesn't wet the floor.

I don't think I'll ever get used to ghosts.

"Tragic?" I manage to say.

The man shrugs. "Nothing cheerful about how the boy died. There's a reason he's called Ebb," the man says. "Used to be Robert when he was alive. Loves animals, that boy. Even bugs, always drawn to them."

I wait for him to say more.

"He's looked after you since you were a baby, as much as a ghost could, which I suppose isn't much. Kept you company even though you couldn't know you *had* company."

I stare out at Ebb, trying to reconcile the boy he's describing with the ghost I've met—angry at me one minute, melancholy the next, sometimes kind and sometimes not.

"Don't mind his moods," the man in the slicker says, as if he's read my thoughts. "You'd be moody too if you were tied to earth while your parents had moved Beyond."

I turn. I want to ask about Ebb's parents, and what happened to them, but before I can summon the words, the man floats through the wall and is gone.

I swivel back to the window and watch Ebb move from tree to tree, whispering to tiny insect ghosts. He must sense me watching him, because he turns and looks toward the window, then lifts his hand in a half wave. I half wave back, blushing with shame for being so mean to him. And then I turn away.

I look around my room, feeling defeated. The first day is already gone, and I'm no closer to finding anything that could help me fight a witch, except for the cryptic note on the back of my birth certificate. I will go to the hospital tomorrow, I decide, though I have no idea what I'll look for. Hopefully Germ can come with me.

I nervously fiddle with my mom's knickknacks on my shelf—the matchbox, the shell-engraved whistle, an old wrinkled Playbill, and then my fingers move to a few of my worn, faded books: *The Wind in the Willows*; *Aesop's Fables*; *M.C. Higgins, the Great*; *Anne Frank: The Diary of a Young Girl*; all the Harry Potter books; and on and on.

My books have sheltered me from the moments that are hard, and whisked me away when I needed to escape. They're like wool that keeps you warm in the cold and cool in the heat. On days when I find it especially hard not to crumple up because I wish I had a different mom or a different life, I escape to them.

Now I read my favorite, well-worn chapter in the whole Harry Potter series, where Ron, Harry, and Hermione make an escape on the back of a dragon they once feared. It's my favorite because I like how by saving themselves, they save the beast, too. I love most of all the moment when they rise up, and fly.

And like always, even in the face of witches and curses, it works. It calms me. It saves me the way it always does.

And I sleep deeply afterward.

And the witch doesn't come.

CHAPTER 13

The phone rings downstairs, waking me with a jolt Sunday morning. Before I'm even out of bed, I'm thinking about time: three days till dark moon. *Three days, three days*, I think with each step down the stairs.

I hurry to the kitchen and pick up our ancient phone from the cradle. (We have an old answering machine, too—all left over from some unknown owner of the house years ago.)

It's Germ. She's out of breath, and her words spill out all in a rush.

"So sorry I didn't call yesterday. After soccer, when I got home, I tried to convince my mom that ghosts exist and told her that we talked to a bunch of them last night. But now she thinks I'm having seizures. She looked it up on WebMD, and it says when you have seizures, you hallucinate. So now she's not letting me out of the house. Like, except tonight for the Fall Fling. She said I couldn't call you because we just 'egg each other on.' She thinks I'm calling Bibi right now."

"You're allowed to call Bibi?" I blurt out, more hurt-sounding than I want to be, feeling betrayed by Germ's mom.

Germ pauses for a second. "Because of the Fall Fling. We have to organize for tonight. Do you think . . ." She hesitates. "Do you think you still might be able to come?"

"What?" I ask. My promise to go to the Fall Fling has completely slipped my mind until just this moment.

Germ pauses. "I know, I know, it's really crazy to ask, with everything going on. It's just . . . I can't back out because of Bibi, and . . . it's going to be a disaster and I'm going to be humiliated. But I know it's not a big deal compared to . . . everything. I know."

I've never heard Germ sound so agitated. She took on ghosts last night with relative calm. Now her voice quivers with fear. I feel a tinge of disappointment that Germ even cares about any of this stuff right now.

And then I think, *If I'm not there to comfort Germ if she does get humiliated, which is fairly likely, who will be?*

"I'll be there," I say, keeping the disappointment out of my voice. "Of course."

I can practically hear her sigh of relief at the other end. "Thanks, Rosie." She pauses. "I did do a bunch of internet research on witches and stuff like that yesterday. But sorting out make-believe stuff from real witches is, like, impossible. There are all these books that say witches don't float. And I read a bunch about the Salem witch trials, which just sounds like people back then were afraid of women who did what they wanted. I'm gonna keep looking."

Behind her, I can hear the news, which she always has on, and then the doorbell.

"Uh-oh, that's Bibi at the door. My cover's blown— gotta go."

She hangs up before saying good-bye.

I sit there for a moment, engulfed in jealousy I don't like and that I wish I didn't have.

Get it together, sweetie, I tell myself.

And then I look at the clock. It's already eleven o'clock.

✦ ✦ ✦

By afternoon, I'm on my bike riding alone to the hospital, in the rain, in an oversize raincoat I borrowed from Mom since I don't have one. I wear my *Lumos* flashlight under my coat for good luck.

I pull off the ramp where I've always seen the decrepit sign that reads SAINT IGNAT SPITA, and wind down a woodsy road. It's deserted, and I wish again that Germ were with me, because she always makes me feel at least 75 percent braver—but I steel myself and keep pedaling. Whenever Germ is afraid, she says she thinks of gummy bears with ketchup on them, and it's so disgusting that it helps. But it doesn't work for me.

In the dim rainy light, I marvel at the loneliness and emptiness of this place. It must have felt to my mom, when she came here to have me, like she was going to the ends of the earth to hide.

I pedal on and on, and it looks like nothing is back here until the moment that, up ahead as I round a bend, the hospital looms up from the woods.

I brake, and catch my breath.

No wonder Homer said this was a dead end.

The building stands in the middle of a clearing carved out from the surrounding woods, its walls jagged and crumbled like old teeth. It looks like it's been in a fire—black smudge marks snake across its white stone. It's covered in ivy and moss, and its doors are blocked with yellow tape, though most of the tape lies sagging along the concrete landing. The building is surrounded by an overgrown field that must have been a lovely lawn once. A few of its windows are boarded with plywood. On one of them there's an eviction notice. In the wetness, mushrooms have sprouted everywhere.

This is the place where I was saved, by a secret. I wish a place could share its memories the same way people do. I wonder what *The Witch Hunter's Guide*, with all its talk of magic, would say about that.

I take a deep breath and walk into the tall grass. The front doors, behind the tape, stand propped open. I step up to the threshold and lean forward to peer inside.

An empty hall with waterlogged papers all over the ground, a few overturned silver trays. I step gingerly inside, wind down the hallway and then through a series of rooms where old bedding lies in drifts against the walls. Broken glass crumbles under my feet. It's clear right away that I'll find *nothing* here—no records, no sign of the lives that used to be lived here. And Homer says none of the ghosts know the answers.

At the back corner of the building, I find the long suite of rooms that once made up the maternity ward. I walk past one room after another, peering in. The rooms are painted white but have gone a dingy gray. After toeing through some trays and cups on the floor of one of the rooms, I find my way through a door and out into a small courtyard.

I wander along the stone pavers, then turn to look back at the empty building behind me. An old broken clock hangs over the entrance. My heart sinks. Whatever saved me that night, whatever secret spared me that might help me again when a witch comes for me, there's nothing here to find.

It's dusk by the time I get home, and ghosts are floating up Waterside Road as I pedal up the drive. The light from the attic window where my mom sits glows like a beacon. There's a circle of ghosts playing cards by the pathway to the front door. There are two ghost children playing tag in the yard. They all nod a wary acknowledgment to me as I move past.

In the parlor I find the knitting lady and the washer-woman already sitting on the couch passing the time, talking about how a ghost they know lost his life to killer bees, and how that compares to dying of typhoid.

Walking into the kitchen to make dinner, I tune them out as they move from one topic to another, and I only vaguely overhear snippets.

"You know, Crafty Agatha, I hear she sucks the meat off children's bones," the washerwoman says.

"No, she doesn't," the knitting lady—Crafty Agatha, I suppose—says. "But I do hear she cooks people in pots. I hear she hides in a big hollow tree with a cauldron hanging from one of the limbs."

I'm beginning to realize what a gossipy, superstitious lot they are—just as Ebb said. When they're not talking about the weather, or each other, they're talking wild theories about witches, the Moon Goddess, and what lies past the pink haze of the *Beyond*. In any case, they sound like they are going on half wild rumor and half fact, and it's impossible to tell which is which.

"She hides inside a volcano in Hawaii," a voice says from the other side of the room. I turn to see that the drowned sailor in the rain slicker is passing through the room, and now he hovers by the couch. "She was left behind by the others because she lost something the rest of them have, some way of getting to their hiding place, so now she's stuck hiding here on earth. I've heard it from several reliable sources." He gives me a sheepish look. "Sorry, little one. I know it's probably unpleasant to hear."

"What do you know about it, Soggy?" Crafty Agatha says.

"Are you talking about the Memory Thief?" I interject nervously, and they all turn to look at me. "The one who was left behind and can't go where the rest of them go?" The two women on the couch look at each other meaningfully. I'm curious. I wish they could tell me where the Memory Thief hides. Then if I ever figured out how to fight her, I could find her before she found me first. Still, I can't tell what parts are idle gossip and what parts are real.

"Never you mind, little one," Crafty Agatha says. "I'm sure all will be well." They exchange another look that says they really don't think all will be well.

Subtle, I think.

Just then, another ghost drifts in and whispers to them, looking at me.

"She was?" Crafty Agatha says, looking over at me with one eyebrow arched.

I sigh. Now, I guess, I'm the subject of the gossip.

"What?" I finally ask.

"Some spirits saw you riding home from Saint Ignatius Hospital just after sunset."

I nod. Annoyed. I don't like everybody knowing what I'm doing all the time.

"Well, it's just, it's a good thing you weren't there at night," Crafty Agatha says. "Hate to see you caught out by the Murderer so far from home. That could just about frighten you to death, I imagine."

My skin prickles.

"The Murderer?"

The washerwoman and Crafty Agatha nod.

"What would he be doing there?"

"Oh." Crafty Agatha waves her ball of yarn in the air. "Well, he's always either there or here. He comes and goes between the two all night long." I blink at them, waiting for more of an explanation, which they finally seem to realize they should give.

"We don't really know why," the washerwoman says. "Only that he does the same thing every night."

My stomach sinks. *Never tell*, the Murderer always says, like he's keeping a secret. Homer said none of the ghosts know anything about what happened at the hospital that night. But what if there were one ghost, I suddenly realize, who's decided to never tell? Could what happened the night I was born, and the Murderer's secret, be linked?

I look toward the basement door, and steel myself to approach it.

"Leave him be, child," Soggy urges me, floating up beside me. "Ghosts have ways of hurting you, no matter what Ebb says. If they're angry enough. Haven't you ever heard of falling chandeliers? Plates flying across a room? If a ghost is angry enough, he can kill. And trust me. That one is angry enough."

I swallow before I take the last steps toward the door.

I open it, and peer down the stairs, then walk down them, one by one.

I look around, dreading the sight of the Murderer, the coal-red eyes, the rash around the neck.

But the basement is empty.

He's not here.

CHAPTER 14

M y mom drives us to school that night. I only have to remind her once or twice why we're going, while she nods like Germ is some vague acquaintance I've barely mentioned before. The rest of the time, we're silent. And the farther we get from the house and the sea, the more she fidgets and rubs her hands against the wheel.

As we turn onto Main Street, I pause at the sight of several ghosts hurrying to cross the road, dressed in suits as if for work. In the school parking lot, a ghost mother and child drift across the pavement, the mother dragging the child as if he's late for school. Mom drives right through them, though they don't seem to mind or veer off their path in any way.

I take a deep breath as we climb out of the car, then cross the lot and step through the double doors of my school. Only when I'm standing in the hallway, surrounded by crowds both living and dead, does it really sink in what kind of a night it's going to be.

Seaport Middle School is 102 years old, and it has the ghosts to prove it. A handful of dead children float up the hall, yelling so loudly, I can barely hear anything else. A translucent teacher in a long dress shushes me as if I'm the one being loud. A ghost custodian is lying on the hallway floor.

The crowd of living parents and kids meandering through the hall and buying their tickets and fundraiser candy is oblivious to all of it. They walk right through the ghosts, discussing dinner and grades as luminous shades of the past surround them.

I try to paste a look of indifference onto my face, as if there's nothing unusual to see. It's especially hard when the dead custodian lying on the ground turns his head and smiles at me, and his head nearly comes off. How strange it is that the world goes on as usual—with announcements and basketball tryouts and algebra—when the past circles all around us. I walk faster, my mom shuffling along behind me.

I catch a glimpse of Germ as we make our way to the bleachers. She looks out at me as she climbs the stairs to backstage, then glances at a ghost boy who's being particularly loud, and rolls her eyes, exasperated. She's pale and putting on a brave front. In fact, she looks panicked.

"I'll sit over here," my mom says, gesturing to some folding chairs in the far corner of the room. She likes to be away from people—the noise upsets her, and she doesn't know how to make small talk because she has nothing to say. I hurry over to Germ.

"I feel like I'm gonna barf," she says. "Do you think I caught something from Eliot Falkor?"

"I think you're nervous," I offer.

"You're right," Germ says, nodding, her eyes wide and dazed with fear. She blinks at me for a moment, then shakes her head and shoulders, as if trying to shake off the nausea. "What did you find out?" she asks.

I tell her about the birth certificate, and the abandoned hospital, and what the ghosts said about the Murderer. Her eyes widen.

"I wonder what he knows," she says. And then a voice calls her from backstage, and she whips around to listen, then turns back to me.

"I gotta go get dressed."

With that, she hurries up the stairs and disappears through the doors.

I sit beside my mom, looking around. There's a dead referee down on the court, blowing his whistle. And after a few more minutes of waiting, the curtain goes up.

I start a little in surprise when I see that the first two performers are Germ and Bibi, standing there beside each other on the stage, looking very small while they wait for the crowd to go quiet.

The opening act is always reserved for the showstopper. (Usually it's this girl named Lewnyi who's the best at piano of anyone in school.) The other thing is that Germ is wearing a skirt—A SKIRT. The eyeliner is back too, and now there's lipstick.

And then, the act begins.

It turns out, the act is whistling.

They are whistling a medley of show tunes. It all begins slow, with "Singin' in the Rain," followed by "There's No Business Like Show Business." But then they get into more complicated territory: the soaring chorus of "Memory" from *Cats*, the highs and lows of "Send in the Clowns."

I sit there staring, listening, shocked. I didn't even know Germ knew how to whistle. But there she is, her high-pitched trill weaving melodies in and out of Bibi's low harmony, and though they start out nervously and miss a few notes, they are soon careening ahead with a galloping rendition of "Ease on Down the Road"—watching each other carefully as they do it, so that they're perfectly in time. They are so in tune with each other that it begins to sound seamless, like one unit whistling instead of two people.

The whole audience is completely silent. Even the dead referee stops blowing his whistle. Nobody throws spitballs, or laughs quietly into their hands.

And I realize something—I guess at the same time that the rest of the school does. Germ and Bibi are really, *really* good.

When they finish, Germ and Bibi beam at each other and fall into a huge hug, and the crowd erupts into cheers.

And then it happens. Though Bibi's performance was solid, it's clear that Germ's whistling was the breakout piece of the act. And that really hits home when the kids start chanting. It's unintelligible at first, but then I recognize the sound.

They're chanting Germ's name.

CHAPTER 15

When she sees me through the crowd that gathers after the show, Germ smiles and leaps toward me for a hug.

"That was . . . wow," I say. "That was amazing!"

There are all sorts of feelings swirling around in me, but I try to make happiness for Germ be the only one. It isn't that I wish people would chant for me like that one day—I wouldn't like that; it would only embarrass me. But it's hard not to wish they wouldn't chant for Germ, either.

Bibi is right beside her, and for a moment, we exchange a glance—neither of us smiles at the other.

"And you look . . . really nice," I say to Germ.

I do mean it. But also, in her skirt and with her hair done so perfectly, Germ looks like an animal *tamed* somehow. My favorite Germ is the Germ running ahead of all the boys on the playground, hair flapping in the wind behind her as if she weren't going to stop even if she ran off the edge of the earth. It's hard to think of her doing that in a skirt.

The crowd starts to thin, and Germ turns to Bibi as Bibi whispers something to her. They both laugh. And then Bibi steps off into the crowd somewhere. Germ turns to me, her face becoming uncertain.

"Bibi wants me to come to her house and celebrate with some cake her mom made. But . . . ," she says. She looks unsure.

"I thought you weren't allowed out."

"Well, my mom made an exception because of the show; she'd be coming too, to meet Bibi's mom." She looks hesitant, and flushes.

"Bibi is the worst," I say. It just slips out. I think I suddenly understand the term "green with envy." I feel like the color of barf inside.

Germ frowns at me. "I know you and Bibi aren't on great terms . . ." She trails off. "But she said you could come with us."

"I've got to go home and figure out how to save myself from a *witch*," I say flatly.

Germ bites her lip, and her cheeks flush red. She looks like she's going to cry.

"I'll convince my mom she should let me come over to your place instead. Or maybe I could ride home with her and then sneak out. I don't think she's going to—"

"No, that's okay." I sound harsher than I mean to. And then more just comes burbling out. "Go do what everyone else wants you to do. You're getting really good at that."

Germ is stunned for a moment. She opens her mouth to say something, but I never get to hear it. A wave of kids sweeps around us—a loud, chattering group we always said we didn't want to be a part of, and they start to tug at Germ. Bibi clasps a hand around her elbow, pulling her away, as Germ looks over her shoulder at me.

I don't know what to do. I just stand there and watch her disappear out the gym doors. My best friend looks at me once, with an unreadable face—an edge of anger and hurt—but she doesn't fight the current.

For the first time, a shocking thought has popped into

my head and is clinging there, tighter the more I try to push it away. *What if I'm not always Germ's best friend? What if I'm not even her best friend* right now? I've never even considered the possibility—it's like thinking, *What if this arm I've been using all my life to draw and write and brush my teeth with turns out not to be my arm?* And it makes me think of that feeling of having a big missing piece inside. And how if I miss Germ too, I'll be missing, like, three quarters of myself. I'll be, like, one quarter of a person.

I touch the scar on my palm. I worry the line where we once cut and promised each other to be blood sisters forever. But we're not really sisters. We're not stuck together like that—like family. Germ is not really my other half; she's someone who can drift away.

It's a feeling like a hole opening inside, the feeling of a stomach drop as you fall.

Even with what's happened the last few days, it might be the scariest thing I've ever felt.

All the way down the winding cliffside road, looking out at the sea and the sliver of moon above it, I'm thinking I was horrible to Germ and regretting it bitterly. But I'm also angry. I don't understand how anyone could be so excited about what everybody thought of their talent skit, when there are witches in the world.

Maybe it's better this way, I think. Better if Germ stays away so she doesn't get hurt. After all, it's me the Memory Thief is after. But jealousy still grips my heart, and as hard as I try, I can't imagine facing the scariest thing I've ever faced without the person I lean on the most.

As we pull into the driveway, I'm pulled out of my daze by a dazzling sight.

The trees. They're blinking.

Every tree lining our driveway, every tree in the woods surrounding our yard, appears to be alive with light. It takes me a moment to realize why: they are all covered in insects, including what looks to be thousands of fireflies.

"Mom," I whisper, "look."

My mom doesn't respond as we climb out of the car, though she, too, is staring at the trees.

In the air there's a hum, a buzzing from all directions—there are grasshoppers and dragonflies, spinning and flying through the air or gathered on trees, on bushes. Spiderwebs sparkle in the gleam of our headlights. And of course, there, kneeling in the center of the yard, whispering to a handful of regular moths (not the scary kind), is Ebb.

He turns to look at me, almost smiles. Then he gets up and floats in the other direction across the grass.

My heart pinches with regret, and confusion. I look at my mom, who has turned off the car and is still staring at the trees. For a moment I hope she can see the beauty, the way she used to see beauty in everything.

"We should call an exterminator," she says, and turns to head for the door.

Inside, Crafty Agatha knits away silently in her chair. I light a fire in the fireplace because Mom is shivering, but soon she shuffles off to bed without saying good night. I can hear her getting changed and ready for bed upstairs, and the ticking of the grandfather clock on the wall, but otherwise the house is quiet.

Then there is the smallest noise downstairs, a mutter.

I look toward the basement door, and Crafty Agatha speaks.

"He's here," she says. My stomach flops over sickly.

I stare at the door. I don't want to go down. But what choice do I have? I glance up the stairs and wish my mom could come with me. Then I cross the room, wincing at each sound of the floor creaking. I crack open the door, and pull the string to turn on the one dim lightbulb that hangs in the staircase.

Heart pounding, I take the first step down into the dimness. I'm a big giant pounding terrified heart with legs.

I can't see him at first. It's only when I've reached the basement floor and peered in all directions that I spot him in the corner, in the shadows beyond the glow of the light, his red eyes glowing like embers in the dark, his fingers rubbing against each other as if he's holding himself back from lunging for my throat.

"My basement," he says. "My space. My house, my house, my house."

I take two steps backward, but then shakily stand my ground.

"I need to ask you something," I say.

He stares at me, his lips moving as he mutters to himself, but I can't tell what he's saying.

"About the hospital. And the night I was born." Except for his twitching hands, he doesn't move, only watches me. "Were you there when the Memory Thief came that night?"

He stands for a moment longer as if frozen, and then a smile spreads on his face.

It sinks into my heart like a heavy stone. *He knows.* He knows something.

"Please tell me," I whisper. "How was I saved? What

was my mom's secret about the witches? Was it something that helped protect me?"

He chuckles softly to himself.

"Why do you hate us?" I whisper.

He stares at me a long time. "My house, not yours," he says flatly. "I hate anyone who lives in my house."

I stand there at a loss, searching my brain for a way to get him to talk—a way to pull out the secrets that are so close, I can almost taste them.

"But don't you hate witches, too?" I try. "Don't all ghosts hate the witches?"

He shrugs. "Witches are no business of mine. Only my house. MY house."

I look down at my fingers, thinking and thinking. And then it comes to me.

"What if I promised, once this is all over, that I'd figure out a way to get my mom to move out of this house?" To be honest, I'm not sure I can make this happen, but if I can fight the Memory Thief and break my mom's curse, it seems like moving would be the least of my worries.

The Murderer is silent a moment, as if considering, but then he shakes his head. "Don't think so. No. Don't think so at all. Don't believe a promise like that."

I look at him for a long time, and my eyes trail to the mark around his neck. A question pops into my mind.

"What did you do, that was so bad that they hung you? Why do they call you 'the Murderer'?"

In less than a second, the Murderer is moving. He zips toward me, and stops just within an inch of me, and across the room, the axe falls off the wall. His face is in my face, his red eyes boring into mine.

"GET OUT," he hisses.

I back away slowly, to the bottom of the stairs, then run up, taking them two at a time. I slam the door behind me, though I know doors don't help. And I try to catch my breath.

The Murderer is a dead end too.

CHAPTER 16

On Monday, two days till the dark moon, I skip school for the first time in my life. I convince my mom to cover for me. Turns out, it doesn't take much.

"I'll dial," I say, standing by her computer as she punches data from an enormous book of numbers onto her keyboard. "And then you just read this," I say. "Okay?"

Mom barely glances from the screen as she nods. "Okay," she says.

I lay a sheet of paper down in front of her that explains I won't be in today because I have a cold. And then I dial the phone. And though she sounds like a robot as she reads my script to the person who answers, she is polite and unmistakably, at least, my mother.

"Thanks," I say as she hangs up. I give her a kiss on the cheek, and she flinches.

I curl onto the couch with *The Witch Hunter's Guide*, and that is where I spend my morning, looking for anything I've missed.

I read "Secrets of the Earth and Moon," which gets increasingly stranger as I read.

> *There is a magical thread of connection through all things. Most people sense this even if they don't say it. Water, trees, grass, animals, insects, and people are tied together by it, each with gifts to share: water quenches the thirst of the trees, the trees shelter the animals, the animals are masters of motion and flight and song, and the people build worlds beyond what animals can dream. Even the moon has gifts to share—reflecting magical light for people to dream and hope by, its gravity steadying the earth on its axis.*
>
> *But the witches have begun to break this*

*thread, their curses turning people to their
darker natures, causing them to forget, to take,
to grab at the world around them. They want
people to forget their connection to all the other
pieces of the world, and to magic itself.*

*If the witches succeed—and break the
thread that binds us—they can send the
moon and its goddess spinning off into
space. Without the moon, nights will
become unspeakably dark. The earth will
lose the rhythm of its tides. The weather
will grow wild. Witches will be undeterred
by moonlight. Untold chaos will reign on
earth. And people will forget, once and for
all, that they are connected to anything but
themselves. And we will all be lost.*

I sit back, my heart sinking, feeling a deep sense of
dread. I think of how much Germ worries about what she
sees on the news. Are the witches and the world so ines-
capably tied? Is the world really in so much danger?

I flip back to the section on witches and find the Time
Witch—whom Ebb spoke of with such bitterness.

Revisiting Mom's drawing makes my skin prickle and

my hair stand on end. It shows a woman with a hungry mouth and sharp teeth staring out at the reader, dark black circles around her empty blue eyes, the pupils as tiny as pinpricks. She wears an old-fashioned black lace dress and a necklace of pocket watches, but it's her eyes that scare me most. They're deep, limitless, empty—like the eyes of a fish. The first time I looked through these pictures, it was the Memory Thief who struck fear into my heart—but now I feel relief that it isn't the Time Witch who wants me dead. There's a hunger to her and a malice and a deep empty coldness that makes the Memory Thief look meek in comparison.

I read the description of her.

The Time Witch: Most powerful of the witches, besides Chaos. She is catlike, loves to play games and gamble with people.

Curse: Manipulation of time.

Skills: Compresses, stretches, grows, and shrinks time. Makes weapons out of time. Makes people age too fast or takes away their

*ability to grow older. Makes happy moments
last less time and sad moments last more.*

*Familiars: Hummingbirds, distinguishable by
their empty blue eyes. They steal, distort, and
warp the time surrounding their victims.*

*Victims: A person cursed by the Time Witch
might age rapidly, or age in reverse. They
might lose entire years without knowing
it. Ghosts, fairly or unfairly, blame the
Time Witch for their own angst-filled
relationship with time.*

The shrill sound of the phone startles me, and chills race up my spine. I sit still, not answering, and wait for our ancient answering machine to pick up.

Germ's voice rings out after the beep. She must have finagled access to someone's phone at school.

"Rosie, it's me. If you're there, pick up?" I stay where I am, frozen. For some reason, I can't bring myself to pick up. I suppose it's a mixture of hurt and protectiveness. The more danger I find in the world of witches, the more I want Germ to stay away. And the more I think of Bibi, the more I want to hide from Germ.

"Why aren't you here today? I hope you're okay. I have stuff to tell you. I'll call you when I get home."

After she's hung up, I turn back to the book, and read the last few lines of the "Secrets of the Earth and Moon" section.

If the grass and the animals and the trees have gifts, people have their own part to play too . . . their own gift.

Imagination is a piece of the hidden fabric that only humans can wield. Imagining is to humans like flight is to birds. It is faint and invisible and hard to see at times, this gift—just a shimmer in the human heart. And it's the reason why witches have always hated and feared us. It is our deepest power.

The hearts of witches are fearsome, and have been unstoppable for as long as time. But do not count out the human imagination. It's a whispering, quiet thing, easy to drown, easy to kill.

But it has a power that can destroy the
most terrible darkness.

I trace the words with my finger. I don't understand it, or what it could mean about how to fight.

But when I close the book, I'm convinced. The world needs witch hunters. It needs people like my mom—or who she used to be—who are brave enough to do what she did. I'm just not one of them.

I'm in my room at around three, staring at the walls and lost for what to do next, when I hear gravel crunching in the driveway and see Germ riding her bike up to the house. She must have raced over from her house as soon as the bus dropped her off.

I step back from the window, and listen to the sound of her feet as she clomps up the stairs and knocks. She waits, then knocks again. Upstairs my mom stirs, but she never answers the door if she can help it.

Germ walks around to the side of the house and taps on the parlor windows.

"Rosie," she calls up to my window, but I don't answer. "Rosie, are you here?"

I tighten my hands around the cover on my bed. I want to hurry downstairs and open the door, but I stop myself. I'm a swirl of confusing feelings—anger at her, guilt about being angry, wanting her to stay safe and away.

After a while, Germ yells again. "Okay, I'm going!" she yells. "But I left some stuff by the front door."

I hear her feet crunching across the gravel a few moments later, and step back to the window just in time to see her pedaling down the driveway and disappearing onto the trail that runs between her house and mine through the woods.

Once she's gone, I walk down the stairs, open the front door, and find a pile of papers held down by a rock. On top is a note in Germ's big, messy, greedy-for-the-page writing:

> Found some interesting stuff
> at school and printed it out.
> I figured sometimes the
> internet might know more than
> ghosts do. Hope this helps.

I take the pile inside and sit down on the sofa, sifting through what turns out to be mostly printed newspaper articles, all about—for some reason I can't guess at first—a man named Hezekiah Thomas. He lived in Seaport in the

1920s and was hanged following a strange and sad saga. I become more and more riveted as I read.

The saga begins with a woman named Helen Bixby, who moved to town when Hezekiah was twenty. He fell so in love with her that he learned carpentry and built her a house with his own hands as an engagement gift. Only, Helen Bixby turned him down and married someone else—and then lived happily with her husband just down the road, Hezekiah's only neighbors.

The tragic part comes next. One night, Helen—her husband away for work in the city—showed up at Hezekiah's house in a blizzard. She was having a baby and it was coming very early, and she needed help getting to the hospital. Hezekiah, seeing her outside and consumed with bitterness, ignored her cries at his window, the sound of her fists pounding at his door. He watched her wander away in the snow. Helen Bixby, I read on breathlessly, never made it to the hospital; she died in the snowstorm.

And then I come to the part that really makes me pause.

The articles indicate that no one would have been any the wiser about the terrible thing Hezekiah had *not* done if he hadn't—drunk on whiskey one night—confessed all of this to his brother, who turned him in. And he was hanged for his crime, though many said it wasn't a crime at all. One of the headlines of the articles reads: WHAT MAKES A MURDERER?

My arm hairs begin to prickle at the words.

I shuffle now, fast, through the articles until I come to one with a clear photograph, one that I can make out more easily.

There is the photo of Hezekiah Thomas. His eyes are fiery and full of anger. His skinny frame is coiled as if he'd like to lunge at the photographer. He is standing beside a beautiful white house, built by his own hands. *My* house.

I know him, of course. His face is only too familiar to me. He lives in my basement.

He haunts the hospital because he should have brought her there that night, I think. *He can't let the past go.*

I feel a small—just a tiny—prick of sadness for the Murderer. Clearly his guilt and rage have made him a monster.

The phone rings again; again it's Germ, and I don't answer. She calls a few more times, then gives up completely. As the afternoon fades into evening, the house is quiet again.

Watching the sun sink slowly in the sky, I feel a weight in my stomach—about the Murderer, about the witches, about my mom. All of this knowledge, and I'm no closer to really knowing anything that can help.

Is Ebb right in telling me I should go, leave, run away and never come back?

I walk to my closet and pull my orange backpack out. I start to think about what to take if I do leave—I lay aside a couple of books, some warm clothes, a bag of Twizzlers I keep in my drawer. I put it all in the backpack, just in case.

Downstairs I make dinner for my mom and me. The wind is blowing, but clouds only briefly cross the moon before they float onward. The sound of the wind whistles against the windows.

"Some say the wind is the goddess, trying to blow the world's troubles away," Crafty Agatha says abruptly, startling me. I hadn't realized dusk had arrived. "Sometimes it feels like she will never stop."

I follow her eyes to the window. I don't see—at first—the lonely, forlorn figure floating along the edge of the cliffs, surrounded by fireflies. But then my eyes and attention focus, and I realize I'm looking at Ebb. I bite my lip for a moment, then—suddenly decisive—pull my coat on, slip my trusty flashlight around my neck, and hurry outside.

I catch up with Ebb by the cliffside. The ghost of the rabid possum is out tonight, and he nips at my heels viciously as I walk, before he finally hobbles away. The wind is wild, whipping at the bugs and the grass and the trees, but Ebb doesn't seem to notice. Still, he's a lonesome sight.

When I reach him, he's talking to a grasshopper on a leaf.

"What are all these bugs doing here?" I ask flatly. I'm not the best at starting conversations. A *hello* would probably have been better.

He looks at me for a moment, and I worry, since I've been so rude to him, that he's going to ignore me. But he finally says, "They came to get a glimpse of you. Insects spread news pretty fast." He shrugs. "They came to see the girl they think is going to fight witches and save the world."

I shake my head. "One witch," I say. "And why do they care?"

Ebb takes this in, then looks down at the grasshopper again. "Animals, insects . . . they see the invisible world much easier than people do. Like, you know how dogs seem to be barking at nothing sometimes?" I nod. "It's not nothing. Anyway, animals hate witch darkness as much as anyone else does."

I watch him. "How do you talk to them?"

"It's mostly listening, really. When you're dead," Ebb says, "you can't make a sound that the living will hear. You learn to listen instead."

Ebb pulls his ghost spider out of his pocket, and gently pets the creature on the head with his pinkie. I try not to stare.

"I don't understand," I say. "Like . . . what would a tree even *talk about*?"

Ebb shrugs. "Oh, I dunno, bird nests, the weather, wind, earthworms tickling their roots, what the soil tastes like on any given day, when their bark feels dry. Stone is the hardest to understand—very slow to say anything, pretty aloof, concerned with ancient news—volcanoes, floods long ago. Mosses are kind of interesting." He tilts his head thoughtfully. "Constant gossip about when it's going to rain. Nature's always talking, if you know how to hear it."

I think of what *The Witch Hunter's Guide* says about nature and magic, how it's all connected.

I look around, and my eyes settle on a small cedar tree at the edge of the property where the land plummets down to the sea. "And what's that tree saying right now?" I ask him, fighting back a smile, the first I have smiled in days.

"It just keeps pointing its branches to the water. All the trees in the yard do. Like they're trying to tell us something. But I can't figure out what."

Words rise into my mind. *He's out there swimming, waiting for me,* I think. But I shake the thought away.

"Have you had any luck," Ebb asks, "finding more clues?"

I tell him about the hospital, and the Murderer, and everything I've read in my book, and how none of it has led anywhere. The more I talk, the more my frustration and worry tumbles out.

"I still don't even know how a witch weapon works," I say. "I still have no idea how to find one. I'm completely defenseless, which means I'm no closer to finding out how to kill a witch."

The wind is blowing so hard, my hair keeps flying into my mouth as I talk. Ebb looks at me shivering, then up at the sky.

"Let's go somewhere away from the wind," he says finally. "I want to show you something."

Ebb leads me down the path that crisscrosses down from my high yard to the beach, winding through rocks and steep crags.

"Where are we going?" I say, looking up at the cliffs all

around us, feeling nervous the farther we get from home on such a wild night. Far above, the cloud shepherds are busy herding shapes of mist. Ebb's answer doesn't exactly reassure me.

"Better just see it when we get there. It'll sound too creepy otherwise."

Still, I follow, scrabbling clumsily down the steep rocky trail as Ebb floats easily ahead of me. We emerge onto the beach, at the edge of a cave Germ and I used to explore when we were younger.

He leads me to the lip of the rocky hollow, and we hurry inside out of the wind.

"Don't worry. High tide won't be for a while," he says. "If there's one thing I know now, it's the tides."

I turn my flashlight on and look around. It's a dismal place—dark and empty, musty, mildewed and forlorn. Ebb turns to me, looking almost embarrassed.

"Where are we?" I ask. But with a sick thud in my chest, my eyes light on something that gives me the answer before he can.

On the wall of the cave, just visible in the beam of my light, are words etched in stone: *Here on this day May the 5th, Robert Alby and his parents were taken by the tide.*

Ebb clears his throat. I realize, in a sudden flash, how a Robert might come to be known as an Ebb. How *ebb* is what happens when the tide goes out.

"This is where I died," Ebb says, looking everywhere but at me.

CHAPTER 17

"I used to use this place as my hideout, back when I was living. I called it 'pirate's cove.' I loved to come down here and look for fish and shells and sea critters. That was eighty-seven years ago. . . ." His voice trails off for a moment.

"The afternoon I died, I'd caught this spider in a matchbox and named him Fred." He nods to his shoulder, where Fred is now perched as if listening raptly to us.

"It was such a hot lazy day. I didn't mean to fall asleep.

I just lay down on that ledge over there to rest my eyes for a few minutes, enjoy the coolness of the cave."

Ebb pauses a long time.

"I woke to cold water lapping all around me, the waves crashing in too fast and hard for me to escape. I screamed for my parents. I guess they were out in the yard above, because somehow they heard me. They tried to rescue me. But none of us made it out. Not even Fred." He reaches for his shoulder, and strokes the spider gently.

"My parents, they moved Beyond right away. One minute we were all waking up as ghosts, looking at each other, trying to understand what had happened. The next moment"—he looks up and out of the cave—"they were surrounded by pink sparkling dust, and then they were gone. I was left behind, stuck here on earth. That's how it is."

I feel such sorrow for Ebb. To spend eternity tied to this lonely hole by the sea and a house that used to be his. I want to say something consoling or kind. But as usual, the words don't come when I need them. Being quiet is a hard habit to break. When even your mom doesn't want to hear about you, you learn that your feelings have nowhere to go but in.

"I used to fantasize that I could learn from your mom—

to hunt the Time Witch. That maybe if I could hunt her, I could make her give my time with my parents back. But I've learned over the years—we ghosts hide from witches; we don't fight them." He hangs his head.

"Why do you think you didn't go with them?" I ask.

Ebb shakes his head. "I know it's different for every ghost. The Beyond, and what ties us here, is such a mystery. But I think . . . I caused something terrible to happen, and I need to cause something good to happen to make up for it—I've believed that for years." He dims and glows, like a ghost blush, as he looks at me. "I always thought if I could protect you, like I didn't protect my parents, maybe that would be it. But if anything, I helped get you in trouble in the first place. And also I just want you to be safe." He blushes again.

As he speaks, something catches my eyes in the dim moonlight that filters into the cave. Ghostly spiderwebs. Hundreds of them, sparkling in the moonlight like fine, delicate strands of silver. The webs are glowing—luminous webs made by a luminous, ghostly creature. They are beautiful and strange, delicate and miraculous.

But the strangest thing of all is that they've been—impossibly—spun into *words*.

*"Burp," went the bat. And out came
a galaxy, the inhabitants of which never
learned that the bat that burped them out
had ever existed.*

*"I'm Higgle Piggle, the Elf in the shoe,
and I'm going to give your breath back to you."*

"Hey," I say as a strange recognition slowly dawns on me. "Those are words from my stories."

Now Ebb practically turns supernova bright, a massive blush.

"I taught him," he admits, gently cupping Fred from his shoulder and depositing him at the center of one of the webs.

"Taught him my stories?"

Ebb glances away, embarrassed. "Yours, and lines from the books you read too. He likes the words. *I* like them too. They . . . help me."

"What do you mean?"

Ebb thinks for a long time, looking sheepish, before continuing.

He sighs. "All I know is, my afterlife was pretty glum until you showed up in the house. Even as a baby, you were quiet, but full of something *bright*. Then you got older and started writing your stories, and I read them over your shoulder. And . . . well . . ." He looks at me, at a loss as to how to explain. "There's so much to be afraid of," he goes on. "Even the world's sweetest, most innocent things are not safe from witch darkness. But your stories always made me feel like it was possible that everything could be okay somehow."

Now it's my turn to blush. I don't know what to say. I think of all the times the books in my room have helped *me* when I felt sad or lost, and to think that my stories could do that for Ebb feels strange, and good. I feel deeply embarrassed and warm inside. I reach out toward one of the webs, and just barely touch it. There is something so beautiful and delicate about it, fragile but strong somehow.

"I'm sorry for kicking you out of the house," I finally say. It's a big step for me.

Ebb nods. "It's okay. I understand."

"I guess we both just want our parents back," I say.

Ebb nods. "I want to be in the Beyond with mine, and you want to be here on earth with your mom."

"Tomorrow is only one more day till the dark moon," I say, turning glum.

Ebb looks at me for a long time. "I suppose you're not going to run," he says, sounding resigned.

I think of my packed backpack, then shake my head. I know in my heart I couldn't bring myself to leave, to give up.

Something seems to move across Ebb's face, some kind of choice being finally made. "Then . . . I have something else to show you," he says.

He moves toward the back of the cave, and gestures for me to follow.

"I'm sorry I didn't tell you before," he says. "But I wanted you to run instead of giving you false hope." He pauses and looks at me. "If you're staying, you're going to need it."

He leads me back deeper into the cave, to a little nook completely protected from the water, where only something smaller than a boy could fit. Then he turns to me very solemnly.

"I'm not the only person who used this cave as a hiding place. Someone else did too, many years after I died."

He nods me forward, and I look inside. I can't tell what's in there, so I pull it out. It is heavy in my hands.

"I don't know how it works," Ebb says in a warning tone.

I unwrap whatever it is from the bundle of cloth. And gasp.

It's a quiver full of arrows, and a bow, but it's also unlike any bow and arrows I've ever seen—like a weapon, but also something *more*. Each arrow is painted with tiny, exquisite scenes: forests and flowers and sunsets and dreamy landscapes. The bow, too, is covered in brightly colored depictions of rainbows and fields and mountains. The paint is faded, but I would recognize my mom's art anywhere.

And though I have no experience in these kinds of things, I realize what Ebb has been holding back.

And I know a witch hunting weapon when I see one.

CHAPTER 18

If my house is isolated, Germ's is almost impossible to find. It's not on GPS or any maps because it's not really supposed to exist. Her dad, when he was around, parked their mobile home there because the land was unclaimed and it didn't cost anything, and they just . . . stayed. It's like the house that isn't, tucked behind an old junkyard.

Tuesday afternoon, one day till dark moon, that's where I go, breaking my promise to myself about leaving Germ out of things.

I do this for two reasons: One, I can only stand not talking to Germ for so long; forty-eight hours is about the maximum. Two, if anyone can teach me how to shoot a bow and arrow, it's Germ, who never met a physical activity she wasn't great at. I once saw her do a front handspring in gym class, her heavy frame flipping deftly end-to-end, simply after watching someone else do it *one time*. She can ski backward. *I need her* for this. And, I reason to myself, it doesn't involve her fighting a witch, only her helping me figure out how to do it myself.

Above, the sky is so overcast, the clouds look like a wet soggy web. Worried that we could be in for a dark, moonless night, I bundle the bow and arrows into my backpack (they poke out the top, but I wrap them in an old towel) and climb onto my bike.

I steer into the woods—down the well-worn path between Germ's house and mine. As I ride, I keep thinking about last night and everything Ebb told me. I keep coming back to something he said about his death—that he feels like he was responsible for something terrible, and now he needs to do something good to rectify it.

It's not just the sadness of the story that clings to me. It's that it feels like it *means* something important, but I can't quite figure it out. The meaning is out of my reach, something that keeps slipping my mind.

A few dragonflies follow behind me as I go deeper into the woods. As I pull up at Germ's, I leap off my bike and lean it against the usual tree, and on second thought, tuck the bow and arrows behind the bike in case Mrs. Bartley is home from work early. (Usually she works till long after dinnertime.) Germ's brothers do sports after school and are rarely home before seven.

Germ thinks her trailer is shabby, but I've always loved it because it's overflowing with her and her mom and her loud and unruly brothers. Today the sight of it makes me nervous as I climb the stairs. Usually when I need to apologize but can't find the words, Germ says, "Let's pretend we already did this part," and all is immediately forgotten. But this—Bibi West and how Germ is changing and I'm not—is bigger than any fight. It's not something that can just go away. And that's something new.

I knock, and wait. After a minute the door opens and Germ appears. She looks unsure whether she's happy to see me. A hint of a smile flashes across her face, but then it moves aside for anger, and also, maybe, uncertainty.

The gulf between us feels wide. I wonder, with a feeling like an astronaut floating in space, if it might even be unfixable. I swallow the lump in my throat.

"I have something to show you," I say.

We are standing over the bow and arrows, which I've laid on Germ's bed.

She stares at them for a long time.

"Why're they painted?" she asks.

I shrug. "I don't know. *The Witch Hunter's Guide* . . . the women who hunted witches in my family, their weapons . . . they all involved beautiful things, music and embroidery and stuff. I guess it's connected to that somehow."

Germ takes it all in, looking hesitant. "Well"—she nods to the bow and arrows—"*does* it work?"

She looks at me. I look at her.

"You haven't *tried* it yet?"

"You know that if you don't help me, I'll end up hitting the nearest person within a mile and killing them."

Germ thinks on this, and nods. "That's true," she says. "But, Rosie, dark moon is tomorrow." She heaves a sigh. "You've got almost no time to learn."

"I don't have a choice," I say.

We go out into the yard, which is really just scraggly woods all around the trailer. Germ selects a big old dead oak tree as the target. Dusk is falling quickly. I hold out the bow and arrows to her to try first, but she shakes her head.

"You're the one who's good at this stuff," I say.

"But you're the one who needs to know how to hunt witches," she says.

"*Witch*, not *witches*. *One* witch."

Still, I guess she's right that it has to be me. At the same time, if all that's standing between me and a witch is my athletic abilities, well . . . I try to push the thought out of my mind.

Germ helps me get my stance right, back leg facing forward, front leg bent slightly to ground me, arms strong.

I'm pretty sure we both expect this to be the first of about a thousand tries to hit the tree.

But things do *not* go as we expect.

The arrow veers far wide of the tree—that much isn't surprising. It sails in the direction of Germ's brother's junky old car, which he saved all his money last summer to buy. It's going for the windshield or the hood or the front right tire, depending on how fast it spirals downward.

But as it's flying, something miraculous happens. A shimmer—a puff of something—appears, filmy and delicate but unmistakable, like the trail of exhaust you might see from an airplane. Only this is in a wave of colors and small, diaphanous shapes so exquisitely beautiful, so full of light, so warm and clear and sparkling that just looking at it makes something feel better inside you. The shapes are the shapes my mom has painted on the arrows; the colors are my mom's colors come to life—as real and unreal, at the same time, as ghosts. They shimmer in the air for a moment, then disappear.

I turn to Germ just in time to see the same look of awe on her face a moment before the arrow hits its mark, landing with a *thwack* in the car's front tire after all. There is a loud hiss as the tire loses air.

Germ says two things.

"Well, that was something."

And then,

"David's going to kill me."

We practice for two hours, until my arms feel like they're going to fall off and I can't feel the pads of my fingers. When I want to give up, Germ makes me practice some more while she runs little circles around the yard and picks up the spent arrows. We take a break for dinner, and then we start again.

For a while, the beautiful shimmering trail of color flies out behind the arrow each time, but it gets dimmer and dimmer. Soon, it stops appearing altogether, which worries me.

"Maybe witch weapons have to rest," Germ says.

By seven p.m., after about three hundred shots, I've hit the tree a total of four times. Still, three of those are in the last twenty tries, so I'm getting better. At this rate, if I practice all day again tomorrow, I should have a 20 percent chance of actually hitting the witch when she comes for me tomorrow night. As long as she stands as still as an oak tree, I guess. It's not great odds, I have to admit.

Finally, spent, we lounge on the metal landing outside Germ's front door, which all the Bartleys jokingly call "the veranda," and drink Gatorade. We are quieter with each other than usual. Sometimes when we lie out here, we pretend to talk with our feet, so not talking with our feet is another sign that something is off. I know we are both worried about our friendship, underneath all the other things we are worried about. And what I really want to say is that I just wish things could always be the way they have been for us. But I don't say that.

Instead I tell Ebb's sad story to Germ. I tell her about my failed conversation with the Murderer, and how I even thought of running away before Ebb took me to his cave last night.

"Do you think the arrows can really hurt the Memory Thief?" I ask, thinking out loud. "I mean, they just make a kinda weak puff of colorful stuff. Even if it's a magic puff."

"Puff the magic puff," Germ says listlessly. She's lying on the one decrepit, strappy outdoor chair, with her legs dangling over the arm. "Maybe it could, though. Maybe you just have to hit her one time. What if you get her with just one arrow, Rosie, and all your troubles are over?" I think about this, but it's too hard to imagine.

"I wish we knew where she was hiding," she goes on after a moment. "It's weird to sit and wait for you to be attacked."

Something nags at me.

"There's this giant piece missing," I say. "I still don't know what happened the night I was born. There's some big part of the whole picture that I can't see, and it's important. I know it is. The thing about someone out there swimming, waiting for her, and how it's tied to that night."

Germ nods slowly, thoughtfully. "And I guess that's the one thing the Murderer won't tell." She runs a hand through her thick blond hair. "He's not really the kind of person to do a good deed."

I loll a lazy, tired foot in agreement. And unbidden, my mind drifts back to Ebb—to the things he said about his parents, to his own wish to do a good deed to cancel out a bad one.

And I sit straight up.

"Unfinished business," I say.

Germ looks at me in surprise, confused. "What?"

"It's something Homer said about moving Beyond. And then Ebb was saying he feels like if he can just save someone—just one person—he can cancel out his guilt for what happened to his parents."

Germ squints at me, not quite following.

"What if it's the same for the Murderer?" I say in a rush. "What if, if he helps me by telling me his secret, he makes up for the person he didn't help? And what if that could let him move Beyond? Every ghost wants to move Beyond, more than anything else, don't they?"

Germ, catching on now, smiles.

"I've gotta talk to him," I say, standing up and moving quickly toward my bike, feet crunching in the dry leaves.

Behind me, Germ hurries to her bike too.

"You can't come," I say.

"It's just talking to a ghost," she says. "It's not mortal combat or anything."

And because Germ can be as stubborn as I can, I don't argue.

We pedal into the woods and ride for home, and the Murderer.

CHAPTER 19

When we get to my house, Ebb is just arriving for the night, floating across the lawn with Soggy and Crafty Agatha. Seeing us, he brightens and floats over.

Behind him, bugs are everywhere—swarming the trees, the grass, all over the tree trunks. There is such a huge number of them that I can hear the sounds of millions of tiny mouths devouring the leaves, the pitter-patter of thousands of minuscule feet, possibly even the sound of bug poop falling.

"What's with the bugs?" Germ asks as Ebb approaches us.

"They think I'm gonna fight witches and save the world," I say.

"Oh," Germ says flatly.

"We're looking for the Murderer," Germ explains to Ebb as he reaches us. "Is he here?

Ebb glances over his shoulder, and then looks back at us and shakes his head.

"He's not with us tonight. He went the other way."

I nod. "To the hospital?" I say. "We'll go find him there."

Ebb looks uncertain, then looks up at the sky. "I don't know if it's the best night to go looking for the Murderer or anyone else. So cloudy tonight, the moon is blocked. It worries me. What if . . ."

But I'm already climbing back onto my bike, because it's too important to wait. And before Ebb can finish, Germ and I are careening down the driveway and barreling onto Waterside Road.

"Be careful!" Ebb calls to us helplessly from the driveway, and I cast one look at him over my shoulder and nod before we vanish behind the trees.

Within half an hour we're on the lonely, woodsy road to Saint Ignatius. I've clipped my Harry Potter *Lumos* flashlight into a place I made on my handlebars to act as a headlight. Patches of fog roll by us as we ride north. Crickets and tree frogs sing from the trees.

Finally the broken-toothed silhouette of the hospital looms up ahead. Even Germ slows down at the sight, her feet going still on her pedals.

In the dark, with the magic fabric visible, the place is transformed.

The yard around the hospital is full to the brim with soldiers—young men in green uniforms, some in much older-looking blue ones, some missing arms or legs, some with bandages around their heads—too many to count. There are also nurses in old-fashioned dresses, doctors in old-fashioned attire, one doctor with a beard all the way to his waist. Scattered among them are a few other patients—women and men in civilian clothes, but not many.

The night is growing dark, but the gathering of ghosts casts a glow big enough to light the whole hospital. They all turn to look at us as we inch slowly toward them.

I scan the crowd for the Murderer, but my heart sinks—he's not in the outer yard.

I climb off my bike and slowly walk into the crowd of spirits, trying to look unafraid. Germ follows my lead. The crowd mostly parts for us. Some ghosts we walk through and others move aside. I hold my breath as we make our way in through the decrepit double doors.

The hospital is just as crowded inside. Germ and I thread our way down the halls, looking at every face to see if it's the right one, but no luck.

It's not until we get to the courtyard at the back of the building that we find him. He's alone, floating back and forth outside the windows of the maternity ward, muttering to himself.

Of course, I think. *Of course he wants to be near the mothers and babies.*

For a moment, we watch him through the window, scared to approach.

But then the Murderer turns, and his eyes slide to ours through the glass. He stops floating, and I go completely still with fear. His eyes flame up like coals as they lock on mine.

"I think I'm going to have to do the talking," I say to Germ.

Germ looks over at me and says flatly, almost in despair, "Well, then this will go well."

I lower my hands to grip the door, and step out into the courtyard. Germ follows.

The Murderer grins as we approach. His teeth glinting, he reminds me of a cat showing its jaws to a mouse before eating it.

I take a few steps closer, nonetheless. Behind me, Germ's breath is quick and nervous.

"Terrible night to be out," he says, looking up at the cloudy sky and smiling. "What brings you?"

I take a deep breath and blurt it out. "Helen Bixby," I say.

At the name, the smile slides off the Murderer's face. If he hated me before, his expression now holds something worse. Pure unadulterated rage.

I force my voice to leave my throat, to keep going.

"I think you have unfinished business, Mr. Thomas. And I'm hoping I can help you finish it."

He blinks at me, confusion for a moment dimming the coals of his eyes. I've caught his attention.

"I know you didn't help when you should have, and because of that, a woman and her baby died. I know that's why they hanged you."

He frowns now, rubbing his hands together agitatedly. Behind me, something falls. A bust from the hospital roof.

Germ jumps closer beside me, but for some reason I don't budge. I am too close to everything to be turned away. My heart pounds in my chest. I have to convince him. Convincing him is everything.

"I think once, a long time ago," I say, "you didn't help someone, and it cost everything. And I think that now . . . you have a chance to help me, by telling me a secret. And maybe it will set you free."

I look up at the sky. Even on a dark, cloudy night, the pink haze of the Beyond swims above, dim but there. The Murderer, I notice, looks up too. And if it's not just my imagination, there is longing in that look.

"I need to know what saved me that night. What secret my mom had, to protect me from the Memory Thief. How those things are linked to the sea."

He looks down at me, and his frown is now a sad, lost kind of thing. But then he begins to quake with anger, and another stone bust falls from the hospital roof. This time Germ and I both have to dodge to avoid it.

"You can't save Helen Bixby and her baby anymore," I push on. "But I think you can save me and my mom."

"You don't know that that will move me Beyond," he says. "Nobody knows that. The Beyond does not make promises, or spill its reasons."

I hesitate. I know he's right. And yet, it also feels like

this has to be the moment his afterlife has been waiting for. I just don't know how to convince him.

He looks around. "You and your mother took my house. It's MY house."

"I didn't know it was yours," I whisper apologetically.

His angry quaking slows, but his eyes remain hateful.

I cast about for anything else to say. "This has to be what you've been waiting for. Two lives lost, two lives saved. It evens out. It all makes sense."

He blinks at me for a moment, and strangely everything seems to change. He looks at me, then Germ, then back at me. Suddenly, inexplicably, he laughs.

"Two," he says, then laughs again. "Two lives."

Something about the way he says it makes me feel knocked off balance. He's laughing at what I don't know, and it scares me.

"You were a quiet baby," he says after a moment, turning serious.

I wait.

"It's what saved your life that night," he goes on. "Not any great secret. Not any discovered power."

I blink, wary now, worried. "What do you mean?"

The Murderer shakes his head. He looks up at the sky again, straightens up again. Now he looks solemn.

"They came for her that night," he says begrudgingly. "And they came for the last of the Oakses."

I stare hard at him, chills rising on my arms. The weather is changing, but I barely register it. It's getting colder, the fog thicker.

"*They* who?" I ask. "The Memory Thief? Who else?"

The Murderer goes a little dim, maybe the tiniest bit of fear crossing his face.

"*Two* witches," he says. His eyes widen at me. "*The Memory Thief. The Time Witch.*"

Confused, I'm trying to think what to ask next. But the Murderer goes on, unprompted.

"And they took *him*," he says. "That is the only secret, nothing else. No great power or discovery or secret protection."

Looking at him, I think he must have spoken wrong, but the hair on the back of my neck begins to prickle. Germ, on instinct, reaches for my hand and grasps it.

"Him *who*?" I ask, barely above a whisper. The woods all around us seem to have gone silent. The crickets and tree frogs that were roaring at our arrival are quiet. The moon has disappeared.

"*Three* lives, not two," he says. "And they took *one* to the bottom of the sea."

"I don't understand," I say, shaking my head. I can feel the blood draining from my cheeks. I feel like I'm slipping down a slope with nothing to grab to stop my fall, because of something that has always been *not there*. A missing piece of me. A second half. It all flares up like something my heart knows but doesn't know the contours of.

Beside me, Germ has gone so pale, her freckles float on her skin like in a bowl of milk.

The Murderer just stands there, ruminating, looking up at the sky, distracted. "They took him," he repeats. "Dropped him in the ocean, I guess."

"Him who?" I press. "Dropped *who*?"

He turns to look at me, as if just now remembering I'm there. "Your mother only had time to hide one of you. *He* was crying; you weren't. They never knew there were *two*." His shoulders sag as if in release, or surrender, or both. And then he says the only thing that really matters. "Twins."

Now the sound in the trees is growing louder. Leaves flutter. Insects begin to chirp, hum, and cry. The woods are agitated about something.

But I can only focus on what the Murderer has said. From the moment I hear the words, I know it's true, and a howl rises in my heart.

And then the Murderer cocks his head, as if listening intently to something. Whatever he hears, it makes him turn his face sharply to the woods, and then the sky, and then to me.

"She's coming," he says.

"Everybody, leave here.

"Leave now.

"Run."

CHAPTER 20

Above, a flock of birds takes sudden flight, and flees across the horizon. In the trees, squirrels scurry and leap from branch to branch, all headed in the same direction—*away*. We stand watching them, frozen.

"Um, that can't be good," Germ says.

But I can't think about what I see around me. All I can think about is the word "twins."

"Rosie," Germ says, looking up at the sky, "we have to go. We have to get home. Your bow and arrows . . ."

Germ yanks on my arm, and after a moment I fall into step behind her. But as we launch into motion, I turn my head back to look once at the Murderer. Something strange is happening to him. He is holding out his hands, staring at them. A pink, sparkling dust has appeared around him. He looks at me and lets out a laugh.

This is the last glimpse I have of him—surrounded by sparkling dust and rising slowly from the ground as Germ and I turn away and race across the hospital lawn.

I don't have time to wonder about his fate. I only run.

We're on our bikes within seconds, standing on our pedals and thrusting up the hill. It's so dark, we can't see more than ten feet ahead of us, and that's only thanks to my flashlight.

Heart pounding, iron taste in my mouth, I look up at the sky. If there's a witch out there, it's too dark to see her. I scan the darkness of the trees. I look for the sliver of the moon to show from behind the clouds.

"It's too early," I say to Germ as we pedal. "It's not time. She can't be coming."

Germ casts me a doubtful look as we chug our exhausted legs up the incline. "I think maybe she's going to take a chance," she says.

We take a shortcut past the edge of town, soaring downhill. Germ is like lightning on her bike, but she keeps slowing to wait for me. It occurs to me for the millionth time that she's much more of a fighter than I am.

"Strange weather," someone calls out to us as we pedal past the convenience store. "Be careful, guys."

And they're right. Up ahead, lit from below by the lights of town, clouds are gathering very fast beyond the trees, in the direction of my house. I don't like those clouds. And then, as we round the bend onto the beginning of Waterside Road, something happens that makes my heart falter. A luminous moth flutters past my face, just barely missing me. I watch it flap past—its iridescent, pattern-shifting wings are unmistakable. Germ and I exchange a panicked look.

A few minutes later, another slaps against my handlebars and tumbles off into the air.

The closer we get to home, the more memory moths fly out of the dark at us. We're riding so fast, they only graze us as we whip past them.

We cut left, into the woods, onto one of our shortcuts. Branches slap at our faces, snag and tear our clothes, but we don't slow down. I follow Germ's eyes up to the sky, and gasp. A blanket of magical moths is headed in the same direction as we are. There are thousands now. Some drift down through the canopy of the woods like snowflakes at the beginning of a blizzard.

My legs feel like they're on fire, my lungs about to burst. The woods have started to look familiar now. This tree, that boulder—we're close to home. But then we burst out into the open clearing of my yard. I skid to a halt in the grass and tumble off my bike in shock.

I feel rough hands pulling me up, Germ yanking me to my feet as I gape.

My house is no longer my house. It is covered, every inch, in fluttering, squirming, shimmering moths. Moths blot out the sky and cover the lawn.

In the woods, panicked grasshoppers and fireflies, spiders and crickets and dragonflies, swarm out from the trees and circle the roof.

A flash of light zips back and forth across the lawn, and I see it's Ebb.

From somewhere inside, there's the sound of glass shattering—and a moment later a cloud of moths bursts out through one of the windows. Roof shingles fly across the yard. The front door, as we watch, comes flying off its hinges as a swarm of moths explodes out from behind. The ghosts of the house have scattered onto the lawn, confused and terrified. Crafty Agatha is swirling in circles, uncertain where to go. The washerwoman ambles past us into the woods. So much for my booby traps.

And then I hear a bloodcurdling scream from inside the house.

As I run toward the sound of my mom in terror, she appears in the doorway, hair in a million directions, clutching her heart.

"Mom!" I scream, and run toward her.

And then I see . . . out above the ocean, perhaps a mile away, a shape is coming toward us. It glows purple against the dark.

"Inside!" I yell, unable to think of anything else. But as we turn toward the house, a cyclone of moths, spinning wildly in circles, barrels into the side of the house, and—with a sound like ripping and then a deafening crash—the whole front wall of my house comes crashing down.

We turn to look at the sky. The shape is now close enough to make out, closing in on us fast. The clouds are gathering low behind it.

It's a chariot, streaking across the sky toward us, but it's made of moths, thousands of them all flying together in unison. And holding on to the reins is a figure all in black. She has one hand in the air, and moths gather around her hands like a flame.

The Memory Thief.

"*She's* the *weakest* witch?!" Germ yells. The sound of moth wings is deafening now. My mom cowers by the front door of the house.

I swallow, and turn my attention to the rubble falling around me, my hands shaking. I have to find my bow. Right now.

I pick up bits of rock and splintered wood and throw them aside. *You can find it, sweetie,* I think. *Just focus, focus, focus.* As I do, bugs swirl through the air like a tornado.

Each time I glance over my shoulder, the chariot looms closer and larger, and I feel so scared I think I might vomit. The bow is nowhere to be found.

But just as I'm about to fall back in despair, I spot it: the corner of the top of one of the arrows. I lunge at it and free the bundle from the debris piled on top of it.

Around us, the clouds are moving faster, and for a moment I catch a glimpse of a strange shape in the mist across the grass, before I turn away.

My eyes on the sky, I try to fit the arrow onto the string, but I can't get my fingers still enough to do it. Suddenly Germ is beside me. She grabs both of my hands, hard and steady, and looks at my face.

"You can do this," she says.

But Germ is a terrible liar. I can see by her eyes that she's not sure at all.

Still, I manage to steady my hand enough to fit the arrow.

The witch is descending toward us.

I want to shoot, but I know I need to wait until she's close enough. As close as the oak tree in Germ's yard.

She comes. And comes. And comes.

She is so close now, I can see her sad, longing eyes. She grins at me.

And then, when the distance is right, I let the arrow fly.

At first, it looks to be far off the mark; it arcs up as if it's going to go clean over her head. But then, on its way down, I see it. It is going to hit. It sails downward, picking up speed, and I can't believe it, but it's headed right at her, trailing colored beams of shapes behind it.

Germ grabs my arm. The shot hits its mark.

And then sails right through her and out the other side. Without even slowing her down.

The wind whips as the chariot reaches the ground, and the Memory Thief leaps out—cast in the glow of ghosts circling the yard. She floats toward me with her arms outstretched, her feet zipping across the ground.

"Come with me, little one," she says. "Come forget with me."

I stumble backward, but not before she reaches my shoulder with her hand—just the tip of her finger. I feel her touch, and with it, a deep frozen chill.

The witch slows in the air for a moment. Then the moths around her swarm directly at me, barreling through the bugs surrounding me.

They land on my shoulders, my face, my ears.

Forget, they seem to whisper through my skin—*forget*. I sink down onto the grass, not because I can't stand, but because I don't remember why I should. Beside me, Germ is yelling something, but I don't know what.

Memories float in my head: drinking Gatorade with Germ on the veranda, Bibi West looking at me at the Fall Fling. Each vision rises up and begins to sparkle like dust, then disappears.

And then the moths are knocked back. The wind is whipping. Patches of fog blow toward the trees. It's unmistakable: shapes loom in and out of the fog, though I can't make them out.

The Memory Thief takes several stumbling steps backward. And just as the clouds part far above to reveal the last sliver of moon in the sky, it dawns on me: *The cloud shepherds are helping.*

A stream of dim white moonlight falls down onto the lawn. The Memory Thief lets out a cry, stumbling backward and shielding her face. With a howl of rage she reaches out for the figure nearest her—Crafty Agatha. A cluster of moths swarms Agatha as she screams. A moment later, the moths fly apart—and Agatha is gone.

Across the grass, Ebb lets out a cry.

The Memory Thief leaps onto her chariot, which lifts up and into the sky, and shoots into the air like a star. In another moment, she's beyond our sight.

I lie on the grass, paralyzed for the moment. My head turned to the side, I gaze at the clouds lingering just at the edge of the field—the strange, misty faces looming out of them, looking at me, almost beckoning me. I can hear Germ and Ebb talking to me, but it's like they are far away. I can only focus on the cloud shapes as they float toward the edge of the trees.

I sit up slowly, and look back toward the house at my mom, then up ahead, at the strange patch of foggy cloud. This may be the only chance I will ever get.

I find the strength to stand. And then, I run. I chase the cloud shepherds into the woods.

CHAPTER 21

The thinnest sliver of moon shines down through the trees. I've been walking for a long while, though I've lost track of time. I only know I've wound my way far from the sound of the ocean and deeper into the woods.

A few memory moths flutter along behind me. Every time one flutters close, my shoulder—where the Memory Thief touched me—aches, and so does my mind. But soon I've left them behind. I think I may be cursed, but only just barely, if that's possible.

The patch of cloud that floats ahead of me acts strangely. Whenever I speed up, it does too, and whenever I slow down, it too slows. It *wants* to be followed, but at a distance, it seems. So one after the other, the cloud and I snake our way through the trees.

I'm tired and my feet hurt and my heart feels heavy. And though I'm determined to keep up with the cloud, with every step, I'm thinking about only one thing: *I had a brother.*

Small mysteries click together, now making sense— my feeling of missing a second half, my mom's long days of staring out the window at the sea. *He's out there, swimming. Waiting for me.*

The Murderer said that's where they took him and dropped him in.

And there is one thing I know now, most of all: it was never some powerful secret that saved me at the hospital that night, not any key to undoing witches. It was a mistake. *I* should have been taken, not him.

This is the thought that makes my feet as heavy as lead. I have to force myself to keep going or I'd curl into a ball and never get up.

Soon I can hear the ocean again, louder and louder, and I know I must be getting close to the shore. It's mistier here. The wet air tickles my face, and I squint to see the cloud ahead as it blends with its surroundings.

And then I take a step and nearly fall over as my stom-ach drops out from under me. I am standing on the edge of a cliff overhanging the sea.

I jerk back and steady myself. The cloud has disap-peared ahead of me into the fog. I can't follow any farther.

My hope faltering, I call out, "Hello?"

Nothing but stillness. I begin to panic.

"Please come back!"

Nothing.

I sink down to sit at the cliff's edge.

Don't give up, sweetie, I think.

But the truth is, I give up.

I stare down at the ground between my knees for a few minutes, thinking I'd rather be a blade of grass, an ant, a speck of dirt—anything but a girl who can't save her mom, a twin with a missing half. I've tried my best and accomplished nothing. I've only found more trouble than I started with.

And then I feel a tickle of moist air on my cheek, and look up.

The cloud is hovering inches away from me.

I see a face loom out of it, made of mist—a round face that disintegrates and rearranges into a long and thin face, then into a bushy-browed face, and then it has no eyebrows at all. But every face appears to be a kind one. It smiles at me gently again and again as it changes.

And then a sound weaves through the mist, as if several threads of voices are joining together at once.

"Chin up," it whispers.

The face keeps changing—one minute old, the next minute young.

"Are you a cloud shepherd?" I ask.

"We are we." The voices gather and whisper.

Now the bushy eyebrows are back, over a bulbous nose, and another gentle smile.

"Cloud shepherds don't save people," I say. "But you saved me. Why?"

"We've watched you. We watch everyone. And we took pity. We know you are weary, young witch hunter."

I shake my head. "I'm not a witch hunter. But can I ask you some things?"

"We will answer what we can."

"Did my mom discover a great secret to finding and fighting the witches, or not? Is there any chance my brother is alive? Why didn't my weapon work?" The questions come out in a rush. I can't help it.

The cloud frowns. There is a long silence.

"We're afraid we don't know your brother's fate."

My heart sinks.

"But we can tell you a story. It begins with a lost item. Found by a man. Given to a woman."

I wait breathlessly.

The cloud dissipates, and the face disappears completely. A moment later, a shape rises up before me—a girl, about twelve years old—all made of mist. I know instantly that it's my mom.

Figures appear all around the girl, and by the way they circle and float, I can see they are ghosts. I smile. It's my mom seeing ghosts, and talking to them.

The girl grows. She's now a young woman, climbing aboard a ship. Setting off to search for witches, I guess. A few miniature clouds float in and out of the scene, high above her, with kind eyes watching her.

The clouds rearrange themselves again and again, to show my mother climbing a mountain, walking the edges of a snowy field, walking into villages, talking to people (though I can't hear the words), sleeping in a doorway in the rain—no doubt searching for witches and their secrets. The moments rise up and then drift out of sight. My heart swells with pride in the person my mom used to be.

And then a beautiful ship rises up out of the mist, and

my mom—a grown woman—stands at one of the rails. Across the deck, a figure watches her. A fisherman with a kind, familiar face. My heart flutters because I know this face by heart, even from photos. This is the moment she meets my dad. I reach my hand out and let it drop as it moves through nothing but mist.

The picture vanishes. The face of the cloud shepherd smiles at me again.

Another scene rises up, just briefly. It's my dad, pulling in his nets near a shore.

"Once," the cloud shepherd says, "each of the thirteen witches was given a special whistle—forged for them by the Time Witch to help them travel into the past. The Memory Thief, forgetful as she is, lost hers one night. And your father found it in his nets."

In the scene, my dad stares at something strange and small caught in the ropes of his fishing net. Then the scene vanishes, and another appears.

Now my dad is leading my mom down to a beach under a misty full moon. He opens his hand to her, and shows her what he's found, and my breath catches in my throat. Even in the mist I recognize it. It's the whistle I stole long ago from my mom's room, with the shell engraved on it. The one that sits on my shelf back home.

"How did he know about magic, if he didn't have the sight?" I ask.

"Love gave him the sight," the cloud shepherd whispers. "Love can sometimes make us see what our loved ones do. And so, he gifted her with the magical item he had found. And it changed everything."

I watch as, in the scene, my mom holds the whistle to her lips, and blows. And something rises out of the water. An enormous shape emerges from the waves.

My legs go weak. I take a deep breath.

This is the secret my mom found, I realize, my heart knocking around inside me. *She was never talking about my dad waiting for her, swimming in the sea. She was talking about something else entirely.*

There are three things that I know at once are true:

The sea really does contain the past.

The witches are hidden in it.

And now I know how my mother planned to reach them.

I don't know I'm crying until the face of the cloud reappears, and reaches out a hand of mist to touch my cheek, and smiles sadly at me.

"My dad drowned at sea," I say. "He's never coming back, is he? I thought before, it might be him in the sea, but no. He's gone Beyond."

The face is blinking at me, watching me with concern and kindness. It nods.

"Does he still watch over me, even though he's gone?" I ask.

"That mystery is the beating heart of the world," the cloud whispers. "Even *we* don't know."

I pull my knees up to my chest and wrap my arms around my knees, feeling small.

"Why did my mom's weapon fail?" I ask.

"Simply because each hunter has to use her own weapon, not someone else's. A weapon has to be just yours, and its power is limited only by the boundaries of your own heart."

I take this in. It's something I should have figured out, from reading *The Witch Hunter's Guide*.

"And what's *my* weapon?" I ask.

The cloud seems to shrug.

"Just take your *gift* and combine it with a weapon close to your heart. That's all."

"I'm not really *gifted* at anything," I say. "Just making things up."

The cloud smiles at this, as if I've said something incredibly silly. "Here's what we've seen people make up: Skyscrapers. Countries. Cures. Ships that fly to the moon.

It took a dream to make the first house. The first language. Made-up things make the world." An arm of mist reaches out as if to pat my head, and though I can't feel it, the gesture feels nice inside. "Imagining is a little like the opposite of witches, don't you think? To stretch and grow beauty from nothing at all?"

I am silent for a moment, at a loss.

"I don't think I can figure it out, or do any of this, on my own," I whisper.

"You are not alone," the cloud whispers. "Don't you realize that now? The past and the ghosts and the trees and the bugs and the animals and the moon and the hum of things—that you are connected to all of it?"

The face scrunches up a little bit and shifts this way and that, looking around, then smiles at me. "It's going to rain."

And then, without warning, the face disappears, and the rain falls down around and onto me from above.

And I sit staring out at the sea, legs dangling, like I'm staring off the edge of the world.

CHAPTER 22

I'm trudging home through the darkness just before
dawn, shivering cold, finding my way by following
the shore, when it reaches me—the sound of quiet
voices singing something beautiful and sad, but not in any
language I've ever heard. The closer I get, the more certain
I am—it's coming from home.

Around me the woods are quiet as if listening too. And
when I make my way out of the trees and into the clearing
of my yard, I find what seems to be every ghost within a

five-mile radius, including every ghost from the historic cemetery, joined together in the song.

I see Germ across the yard. When she sees me, she runs across the grass and tackles me in a tight hug. She is covered in dirt and bruises, and her hair puffs out like a tangled mane. I'm sure I don't look so great myself.

"Is my mom okay?" I ask.

"We're all okay," she says. "Your mom's asleep in a pile of clothes and blankets I made in the kitchen. She doesn't have any idea what happened, really. She thinks it was a tornado." She nods back over her shoulder to where Ebb and Homer are sitting together on a log across the yard. "Ebb went to get Homer, but he and the others were already on their way."

She looks at me, waiting to hear what happened in the woods. When I hesitate, she presses.

"Did you catch the cloud shepherd?"

I nod.

"Did it tell you anything important?"

I look at her for a long moment. And then I shake my head. This may be the first lie I've ever told Germ, even with a nod or a shake. But I'm thinking of the whistle, and the shape that rose from the waves. And I decide, I will keep my mom's great secret a secret for now. The witch I'm after is here on earth, hiding somewhere in the now. And that's my only concern.

I look around me at the spectacle of hundreds of ghosts gathered on my lawn. "What are they singing?" I ask. I see that Homer and Ebb are now floating toward us.

"It's a song for Crafty Agatha," Germ says, turning solemn as she follows my eyes. "I guess it turns out that when a ghost is killed by a witch, it's forever. No going Beyond. She's just"—Germ looks down sadly—"been turned into nothing."

Floating up beside her, Homer shakes his head. "We're singing to the moon, in a language even the earth can understand, to mourn her. We're mourning that witches exist at all."

I think of Crafty Agatha, who never bothered or hurt anybody. And my heart fills with rage at all that the witches have done. What could the world be like without them? What if their ugliness and greed were *not* just an inevitable thing? I guess that question is what sent my mom wandering across the earth looking for ways to destroy them in the first place. For once, I can imagine what compelled her so strongly to go.

"Does the singing help?" I ask.

Homer tilts his head thoughtfully. "I don't know why

it helps to just share how we feel, and to sing something beautiful at the darkness, but it does." He clears his throat and wipes a small tear from the corner of his eye.

"How are *you* feeling, my dear? I hear you were touched by the witch?"

"Just barely." I think about the strange sense of memories being lost, yet still leaving their mark on my heart. I think of my mom and how it must feel for her, to have it go so much deeper. "I feel a little . . . empty in places?" I admit.

"You must have the smallest graze of a curse, but manageable," he says. "The moths may pilfer a memory or two here and there if they can get close to you. But you got very lucky, considering." He looks at me a long time, sympathetic.

"Ebb told me what you learned from the Murderer," he says sadly.

I swallow. "Do you think my brother could still be alive?" I ask.

Homer hangs his head gently. Clearly he does not want to give the answer he believes.

"I'm hoping you've put the Memory Thief on the defensive for now. I'm hoping she'll lie low for a while, lick her wounds. She's not used to being defied, and it must terrify her—even if your weapon didn't hurt her. Now that we know the risks she's willing to take, she could return at any time when the moon is obscured. And now that we are dealing with, well . . ." He takes a deep breath.

"To anger the Memory Thief is a terrible thing. But to trick and tangle with the Time Witch . . ." His voice trails off. "The Memory Thief is a force to be reckoned with, but the Time Witch is something else entirely. Some say she's the worst witch of any of them, besides Chaos. If she hasn't heard about you yet, she soon will, and she will be angry. She will play with you like a cat plays with a mouse. She's twisted. Unpredictable." He clears his throat. "It would be madness not to go into hiding now. Obviously"—he nods to the shambles of my house—"you have no choice. I know a ghost in Arizona, in Coronado Cave. She can take you in at first, and help you figure out your next move."

Beside me, Ebb is very quiet. I keep shooting him looks, but he only stares down at his feet.

"We can stay at my house so you can get some rest before you go," Germ offers. "My mom won't mind. We can tell her it was a tornado that hit your house. Would that be okay?" She looks to Homer.

"Well," Homer says, "I think the Memory Thief will be too rattled to return right away, even on a dark moon. I'd give yourself a day, maybe two, to get ready. And then I'd leave as soon as you're able."

"And your mom can stay with us as long as she needs," Germ says.

"Sun's coming up soon," Ebb says sadly, looking at me.

"Oh yes," Homer agrees, looking out at the horizon for the first pink rays of the sun as they snake, just barely, their fingers above the line of the sea.

And a moment later, something strange begins to happen all around us. Tiny, glowing spirits of bugs that were killed in the fray, crushed by falling walls and pummeled against trees—fireflies and dragonflies and crickets and ants—begin to float up from the ground, all tiny luminous ghosts rising and surrounded by sparkling pink dust.

"What's happening?" I ask Ebb, leaning close to him.

"Their spirits are going Beyond," he whispers back.

And now I know for certain, this is what was happening to the Murderer, too. He was moving on.

I lean back and watch in awe as they lift off—hundreds of them, rising into the sky. It is a beautiful, triumphant, and sad thing. I don't want them to go, but I also know they are going to a place where they belong. It's comforting because it makes me feel like the broken things of the world have a place after all, and that they get put back together again somewhere else.

Ghosts begin to trail away to their graves as the morning arrives. Ebb and Homer wave before departing.

Germ and I watch the last of the ghosts of bugs rise into the dawn—a beautiful glowing ballet of tiny spirits.

And I don't believe that any witch darkness could blot out the beauty of them rising.

CHAPTER 23

If Germ Bartley is a force of nature, her mother is a gentle breeze.

Mrs. Bartley is shorter than Germ and rail thin, and is always looking for someone to split a piece of toast with her because she can't eat the whole thing (which Germ finds agonizingly funny). She has impeccable manners, but when it comes to defending Germ, she's so fierce that all the teachers at school are scared of her. She's also no fool—but because she can't imagine Germ ever lying to her, she believes just about everything Germ says. One time Germ and I ate all the ice cream out of the freezer, and Germ told her we must have been sleepwalking, and Mrs. Bartley read a bunch of books on sleepwalking and made Germ do a hypnosis program to break the habit.

So when Germ tells her, after the three of us drag into the driveway of the trailer Wednesday morning, scraped and bruised and disheveled, "Rosie's house was destroyed by a small tornado," she believes us immediately. And when she calls the police, she tells them the same.

A thin layer of ice forms on the puddles in the yard, and icicles dangle from the eaves of the trailer. The trees beyond the junkyard are all covered in a layer of frost that sparkles in the sun.

We are interviewed and poked and prodded by three police officers, an insurance agent, and two medics. If they are concerned by the way my mom barely remembers what happened, they attribute it to the shock.

Of course, after inspecting my house and yard for themselves, they believe it was a tornado too. How else could all that destruction be explained? At one point I do float the idea that something else did it, just to test one more time if there's any hope for help from any adults at all.

"Do you have any police tactics for handling, um, supernatural forces?" I ask. But the policewoman just blinks at me a moment and then has paramedics come to double-check my pupils to see if I'm concussed.

Germ's brothers hover around us, bringing us juice and applesauce and peanut butter toast because that's what they know how to make. It's a nice break from how they usually just torment Germ by licking all the sweets in the house to claim them for themselves. Eventually Mrs. Bartley shoos them outside because it's too crowded. Germ and my mom and I take turns taking showers. Washing the grime off, I want to cry, to think I'm washing away the particles of *my house* and how I may never see it again.

"You and your mom stay as long as you need to," Mrs. Bartley says to me once we've settled in, squeezing my arm. "We love the company." I try to ignore that she's shouting it over the din of Germ and her brothers bickering.

We sleep half the day, exhausted. My mom is established on the couch that night, though she spends most of the dusk outside, staring through the trees in the direction of the sea. Does she remember my brother with the same muscle memory I hope she remembers me with? Or is it the other thing, the rising shape in the waves that the cloud shepherd showed me, that she is thinking of? Is it both?

I have brought my orange backpack, and Germ keeps slipping things into it that she thinks I might need if I run.

"Your mom can stay with us as long as she needs," Germ says as she tucks a pack of tissues into the front pocket, a compass she nicked from one of her brothers into the flap at the front, money for a train ticket she's taken from the savings she keeps rolled into her pillow. "We'll look after her. My mom'll make sure the insurance company handles things. *I'll* make sure nobody sends your mom away. Don't worry about that, Rosie."

I make my bed up on the floor of Germ's room, occasionally glancing out the window at the moonless night. What if Homer's wrong and the Memory Thief does come back tonight, not "licking her wounds" after all? How long would it take for her to find me here?

Germ puts a sleeping bag beside me. When we have sleepovers, neither of us sleeps on the bed. Out of habit, Germ switches on the news.

We listen to the sounds of everyone else going to bed, including my mom. And then we lie in silence in our sleeping bags, staring at the ceiling while the news drones on in the background.

"I think the witch took some memories of us. I don't know—there's just some hollow places in my head."

Germ smiles. "There's always been hollow places in your head," she teases.

"Remember when we used to build little frog hotels out of logs?" I say, after a long silence. Germ nods.

"I still remember that," I say.

For a long time again, we don't say anything. I'm thinking about what the cloud shepherd said about my weapon needing to be my gift. But my mind keeps wandering.

"Do you think, if I leave, Bibi will be your best friend?"

As I say it, I realize what I'm hoping for. I'm hoping Germ will say, *Of course not! I could never have a best friend besides you!* But Germ only sighs. "You're both my friends," she finally says.

"Well," I offer slowly, uncertainly, "it's just maybe you feel like she gets you better now than me anyway . . . now that we're older," I say. This is as close as I've come to telling Germ my true feelings about things, and my heart pounds.

Germ, exasperated, sits up, cross-legged, her face flushed as she looks at me. "It's true, there are pieces of me Bibi *gets* that you don't. And there are a LOT of pieces of me that you get that *she* doesn't." She glances at the TV, and then at the ceiling, then at me, at a loss. "I'm changing. I can't help it. I know you've never really wanted to grow up, or change, or make new friends. I sometimes think maybe it's because you never got to really be a kid, with your mom and everything. Or maybe it's that since you never had her cheering you on, you're afraid to take chances, you know? I think I understand. I do.

"But I just . . . Rosie, I think maybe you can't stop time." She pauses, and corrects herself. "Well, maybe there's some witch who can. But *you* can't. We're growing up; we can't stop it."

As little as she likes to talk about deep things, when she does, Germ is almost always right. She goes on, interpreting my silence the way she usually does—as permission to keep talking. She takes a breath as if to say the thing that's hardest.

"It's just sometimes . . ." She hesitates. "I feel like I have to pick between *you* and growing up. And between you and everyone else. It's not really about Bibi. It's about me and you. I can't promise we'll ever build frog hotels again or things like that. We may not always be like we *have* been."

She looks at me, and tears glisten in her eyes. She feels bad for me, because she's never really been this honest with me about what she thinks. And it doesn't feel good to hear it.

Outside, the wind is blowing and we both look out,

fearful what the night could bring. I pick at the hem of my shirt, lips sealed tight.

Maybe she's right about all of it. I feel my own pride prickle. I could give up almost anything on earth not to have things change with me and Germ ever. And Germ doesn't really understand and I could never really explain it to her. She has her mom and her brothers—they're all stuck with each other. I don't have anybody like that. If Germ's not stuck with me, nobody is.

She looks down at her hands. "It's hard for me, too, you know. Changing. It's like . . . good to have new friends and care and participate—it feels so good sometimes. And then other times, I care too much. I get caught up and worried that maybe I don't deserve all the attention. I worry about what people think in a way I didn't used to. I lose the brave pieces of myself sometimes, and I don't like it. You never seem to lose yourself like that. I'm not as brave as you that way. You don't care what anyone thinks."

"But I want a normal life," Germ sighs. "Like, to go out with people and go to the movies and kiss D'quan maybe."

I make a face. "He eats dirt sandwiches."

Germ looks annoyed. "Rosie, that was second grade," she says flatly. And then we look at each other, and for just a moment, laugh.

She looks at me solemnly once we've quieted down.

"Rosie, I'm here. Whatever comes for you, I'm here—just tell me how I can help, and I will do it. But with the future, like the *future* future, I think we just . . . don't know who we'll turn into. I may just turn into an average girl who likes going to the movies. And if things go well—you'll be off hunting witches."

"I only want to hunt one witch," I whisper.

Germ shakes her head, thinking something she won't say at first. She looks up at the news, and is quiet for a long time.

"It sounds pretty terrible and hard and scary being a witch hunter. But sometimes I see things on the news I wish so badly I could fix. I wish I could fix everything for everybody." She pauses. "I'm not an Oaks. I don't know why I got the sight—if it's a fluke, an accident. But I guess, even though I'm scared for you, I wish I were powerful like you. Maybe I'd be brave enough to give it all up—all my hope for a regular life, to have a chance to make the world better. I don't know—I think in the end I'm too wrapped up in everything else. But not you, Rosie. You may not know it yet, but you're the bravest person I know. You just seem to forget it all the time. Now that you know about the witches, you won't be able to sit back and do nothing. Not ever again. You're too stubborn."

I think about the times when Germ and I have rescued each other. The time Germ got her mom to show up and cheer when I won the library essay prize, because my mom wouldn't get out of bed. The time after Germ's dad's one visit, when we were eight, when I made her laugh through her tears after he'd gone—with stories of his brain being possessed by gremlins. Without Germ to rescue me, how can I do anything at all, much less be a witch hunter? How can I even be a whole me?

I look at her. "There's some things I haven't told you."

Germ sits upright a little. I tell her about seeing my mom and dad—what the cloud shepherd showed me in the mist, how my dad had the sight because he loved my mom. I still don't tell her about the whistle or what it brought. But I tell her the rest.

"The cloud shepherd told me I have to make my *own* weapon. That's why my mom's didn't work. He said I have to make it out of what I'm good at. Take my gift and a weapon that's close to my heart and combine them. I just don't know what that means, really." My thoughts trail to the other secrets, the ones I'm not yet ready to tell.

"I wonder if my mom had time to name my brother before the witches took him," I say.

Germ is silent.

"I'd name him Wolf, and make him match his name, so he could fight them. I'd give him sharp teeth to bite them with and fast legs to run away and a sense of smell to find his way home even if he's worlds away." I look up at Germ, self-conscious. I realize I've lapsed into my old habit of trying to change what I can't by making things up.

"Stories," Germ says simply, looking at me.

"What?"

"They're your gift. I think you need to a write a story you think can overcome witches."

I take this in. I try to picture myself storytelling a witch to death, but it seems about as likely as whistling a ghoul into a marshmallow.

"It's sort of what you already do anyway, Rosie. You try to change the bad things by imagining them differently."

"And what do you think my weapon would be?" I ask. "Even if you're right?"

Germ shrugs. "Mom's got a chain saw in the shed."

CHAPTER 24

When I sit down that night to write, long after everyone—even Germ—is asleep, I come up blank. I chew my pencil and stare at my paper and think about Doritos and where the Memory Thief might be and everything but an idea. What kind of story could hurt a witch? It has to be simple, but capture everything that matters about the witches, everything I feel. It has to tell the truth but also be made up, because those are the kinds of stories I like best. For some reason, I think about birds—how small and delicate they are, and also how they fly, what a special gift they have that no other creature has. Weirdly, it's easier to write about witches if I write about birds instead.

I set my pencil to the paper, and start.

> Once there was a beautiful world full of
> all sorts of birds: cardinals and parrots
> and peacocks and birds you have never
> heard of in all colors. It was a world where
> sometimes baby birds got taken by snakes
> in the dead of night, and nice birds were
> caught by cats, and good birds got sick
> and fell from the sky, and sometimes mean
> vultures won in the end, and sometimes
> mom birds forgot to love their baby birds.
>
> Meanwhile, though there were some
> very terrible birds and terrible things,
> there were also birds who made nests out
> of beautiful shells, and birds who fought
> badgers and rattlers and raccoons for
> their babies and friends at any cost, and
> birds who sang even when they were
> in cages. And anyway, just about all
> the birds—even the most unloved and

underestimated birds—could fly. Every bird could tell you what worms smelled like and which constellations pointed where. Every bird could hear a grasshopper from two backyards away. Every bird contained multitudes.

The point is, the bird world was full of so many bad things. But it was full of beautiful things too.

And there was one particular bluebird, very small, who could not really chirp around birds she didn't know, and who sometimes was clumsy enough to fly right into tree trunks, and her feathers were scraggly, and her mother bird never brought home worms for her, so she was a little starved inside. But this tiny bluebird decided she was going to gobble up all the darkness of the world, grab it with her little beak and devour it. Nobody had ever thought of that before, so nobody had ever tried it. (And there were plenty of birds who thought it was impossible.)

And it was hard, and uncertain—but the tiny bluebird tried anyway, and she

succeeded. By eating up all the darkness,
she made the bird world better.
    And no more bad things happened to
good birds anymore.

I look at the story and feel that familiar feeling of something both made-up and real. I wonder why that feels so good and always has. Maybe it's just like the cloud shepherd said—that a story makes a space in the world that wasn't there before, and that feels like the opposite of witches somehow.

I don't know if it's the story I'm supposed to write, and I don't know how it will work—if it will shoot colors out behind it like my mom's arrows, or do something else. I don't know how to make my story into a dagger or a sword. But for now, even just writing it gives me hope.

I tiptoe past Germ, then out into the den, where my mom sleeps on the couch. It's no small feat to walk through a trailer full of six sleeping people without waking anyone, but I've always been good at being quiet. After bundling into a coat, hat, and mittens, I walk out into the deep moonless night.

I shiver from the cold as I make my way to the shed. I

wish for my flashlight, but it's still attached to my bike—
which I left abandoned back home. So I find my way by feeling through the dark with my hands. I find the chain saw in a
corner next to the lawn mower. I can't even lift it, and I don't
like the thought of trying to use it. I think it has something
to do with the bright red WARNING sticker on it showing a
person accidentally cutting off their own arm. Still, I hoist it
up into my skinny arms and carry it outside. I pull some tape
out of my pocket that I brought with me, and tape my story
to the side of the chain saw. And then I wait. And I wait. I
shiver and wait for the next twenty minutes to see if something magical happens—some puff of color and light.

When nothing happens, I try other things I find in
the shed: an abandoned fencing sword, an old slingshot
David made of wood, a screwdriver. (I'm getting desperate.) Nothing—when I throw it, shoot it, swing it—gives
off any magical color or glow of any sort. I don't try to turn
on the chain saw, but something tells me it's not really my
style of weapon anyway.

I think about *The Witch Hunter's Guide* and what it says
about weapons: *A weapon is as much a part of a witch hunter
as her fingernails or her teeth. It is tied right to her heart, and
that's where she keeps it close.*

I think how the cloud shepherd, too, said it needed to be a weapon close to my heart.

But there's nothing close to my heart in this shed. These aren't even my things. All my things are at home.

And that's where I think I need to go.

I ride Germ's bike since I don't have mine. I'm so tired, I swerve on the path now and then. I pedal the long curvy trail through the woods to my house, finding my way by memory alone, since there is no light. I'm scared that the Memory Thief may be lurking about, but I'm also scared not to figure things out as fast as I can.

When I get to the end of the driveway, I lay the bike down and stare at what remains of my house. Somehow, there is one lamp on in the parlor, though one parlor wall is missing. It casts a shadowy light in the dark night.

The house is half caved in—all the windows smashed, half the roof gone. Furniture, blankets, and clothes lie tangled across the yard. As I walk closer, I find small and familiar things—a broken cookie jar, one of my mom's shoes.

I climb the collapsing front steps carefully. There's broken glass under every footstep. Walking gingerly inside, I jump at the sight of Soggy, sitting in the one upright chair in the parlor (where Agatha used to sit), looking back at me blankly. Down the hall, I can hear another ghost crying.

There's no rhyme or reason to what's been broken or not. A glass vase sits on the kitchen table, but every chair has been knocked across the room. The coatrack is standing, but the corner cabinet's been smashed to pieces. Feathers from pillows lie everywhere.

I make my way across the parlor to the stairs. I test them one by one, trying to be quick but careful.

Getting to my room, I swallow the lump in my throat. Papers from textbooks and school binders are strewn across the floor. I step in quickly and retrieve the one thing I want most from here—the engraved silver whistle—and slip it into my pocket for safekeeping.

My mom's room is even worse off than mine. All her paintings, all her knickknacks and reminders of the old her: destroyed. And then I see the pile of books on her floor, the ones she kept taking back from me, tumbled on top of each other: *Where the Wild Things Are*, *Rapunzel*, *Hansel and Gretel*. I pick up *Where the Wild Things Are* and flip through it, thinking how just a few days ago I looked for answers to fighting witches in its pages.

And then it comes to me: why my mom wouldn't let these books go.

They're all about lost children.

It settles around me; my skin swims with chills.

And I realize . . . maybe my mom has returned to these stories again and again for the same reason why I turn to the books in my room: to fill in the places that are missing, to push back against the darkness that has taken those things. To remind herself—*because* she has no memory—that monsters can be destroyed, and heroes can win, even if it's only pretend. Maybe stories make us stronger because they make a bridge to things we've lost. Maybe stories make powerful things out of broken ones.

"You're not supposed to be here," says a voice behind me.

I turn.

Hovering in the doorway, looking very dim, and grumpier than ever, Ebb frowns at me for a moment. Then a smile lights up his face.

We sit near the edge of the cliffs looking out at the ocean, me in my coat and wrapped in a blanket, and Ebb undisturbed by the cold. The haze of the Beyond is extra-bright pink in the pitch-dark sky, putting on a rare show. I think how Ebb will be tied to my house forever, even if it crumbles to nothing—until he moves on to the pink haze above us.

"So we just need to find a weapon that's close to your heart," Ebb says. "Surely there's something lying around here you can use."

"Believe me, there are no weapons close to my heart," I say flatly, leaning back on my mittened hands, frustrated. "I'm not really a weapon-y kind of person? I *have* bitten a few people."

We're quiet for a long time, and I feel a little shy around Ebb suddenly. Even though he's a dead boy and an older one, it's a little awkward to sit alone with a boy at night. Maybe not for him, but definitely for me.

"Are you going to leave if you can't figure it out?"

"I guess I have no choice," I say.

"Especially with the Time Witch involved," Ebb adds, his face hardening.

"To think of leaving my mom and Germ . . ." I trail off because I can't put it into words, what this feels like. "My mom's already forgotten me. What if Germ forgets me too?"

Ebb is silent, just listening.

"I wish she and I could make a pact, like we did when we were little. To always be each other's favorite person in the world, best friends. But you can't promise stuff like that."

Ebb looks at me openly.

"I doubt you'll ever really lose Germ. Maybe you just don't have to hold on so tight."

He looks full of something he wants to say.

"I'm sorry I brought all this on you. I'm sorry I showed you the witch book, and the memory moths that night. Things would be so much easier for you if I hadn't."

I consider this, then shake my head. "The hidden world is full of all this terrible stuff. But it's also full of incredible things, and bigger than what I knew before. It feels like something I always longed for, to know there was *more* than just what I see around me. As scared as I am, I wouldn't go back to not knowing."

Ebb goes dim, then bright, then dim.

"You were right about my dad," I finally say. "He's not out there. He's just gone."

Ebb leans back, thinking. "With all the magic in the world, some things still can't come back. But maybe it's okay. Because of what lies up there that we can't know."

I take this in.

"I only wish it wasn't up to me to fight," I say. "I just wish someone else could, somebody bigger and stronger and braver than me. But there's nobody else."

Ebb is still and silent for a long while. Then he reaches into his pocket, pulls his hand out again, and lays it over my palm. As he pulls his fingers away again, I see that he's placed something in my hand.

Fred the ghost spider.

I twitch my fingers. I can't feel the spider, but still he sits there—a little glowing speck on my palm. I suppose he manages to perch on me the way ghosts manage to sit on chairs and move across floors—some kind of friction between the real and the unreal, perhaps. But it's such a delicate balance that when I move my hand too fast, he floats through it.

"He can't fix anything for you. But maybe he can give you courage," Ebb says. "When you feel alone. Having him with me always helps *me*, at least. He told me he wouldn't mind."

I slowly hold up my hand, and watch the spider scurry across my palm, then down into my coat pocket.

"But what about you?" I ask.

"The witches aren't after *me*," he says. "You need him more."

I sit quietly for a moment. And I wonder if inside my coat the spider can hear the *beat, beat, beat* of my heart as I realize that Ebb has become my friend—that I've made another friend besides Germ—just when I'm about to leave. Maybe it's hard not to grow and change. Even for me.

"Thank you, Ebb. After this is all over, if I ever get to see you again, I'll give him back."

But Ebb is looking at me strangely.

"A weapon close to your heart," Ebb says. "And you're not a weapon-y kind of person. Maybe your weapon is not necessarily weapon-y either. Maybe it isn't exactly a weapon at all."

We look at each other, and Ebb waits for me to catch on. "What's your favorite tool for fighting the dark?" he asks me. And suddenly I see where he's going.

I stand up, and Ebb follows. I know where I left my bike when we arrived at the attack, but I don't know if it will still be there.

But then, I see it's where I left it—lying on the grass at the edge of the driveway. And attached to the handlebars is my *Lumos* flashlight.

I detach it and hold it in my hands, then look at him. "Do you think it could work?"

Ebb shrugs. "It can't hurt to try."

The night is quiet around us. I wrap my story around my flashlight, secure it with the rubber bands I find in a still-intact kitchen drawer, and we wait. It's not exactly embroidering a dress, or painting arrows, or weaving a net—but I'm only eleven, and rubber bands are the best I've got.

I turn it on, but nothing really happens—just a normal beam of light.

"Maybe we need to let the magic settle in," Ebb suggests.

So we wait for something magical to happen.

Ebb just floats around the yard because ghosts don't sleep. But I start to doze, and dream of the Memory Thief and the Time Witch, huddled over a fire, holding my baby brother between them and laughing.

I wake to a sound of growling nearby, a shape moving toward me across the lawn, jaws open wide.

I let out a cry, jerk back, and—in the dark—grab my flashlight and turn it on, swinging the beam toward the sound. I only realize it's the rabid possum a moment before it happens:

As the beam of my light hits the ghostly little creature, something changes. A shape, small and impossibly fast, shoots right from my flashlight toward the possum like a lightning bolt. It lands on the back of the possum, who lets out a snarl, then explodes in tiny sparks, and disappears.

The next moment the shape from the flashlight is coming back toward me—sailing through the air gracefully, made of bright blue light. I realize in wonder that it's a tiny, luminous bluebird—small and quiet as it perches beside me on the grass. It looks up at me and lets out one tiny chirp.

Ebb has zipped close to me, and now hovers a few feet away.

I turn to gape at him, and he gapes back at me.

He looks at the flashlight, then at the little bluebird perched at my side.

And smiles.

CHAPTER 25

"Well, go on. Use it again," Germ says.

It's the following night and the three of us are together now: Germ, Ebb, and me. We sit in my abandoned living room shivering, staring at my *Lumos* flashlight, which I've placed in the middle of us. The moon is a new, tiny sliver above.

I slept most of the day, exhausted while Germ went to school. And now, with everyone back at the trailer asleep, Germ and I have snuck over here together, bundled against the cold.

I study the flashlight, biting my lip. "I'm scared I'm going to hurt someone with it," I say.

"It probably only hurts bad guys," Germ says.

"*You* try it," I say to her. "You're good with aim and stuff."

Germ shrugs, picks up the flashlight, points it at a wall, and turns it on. But it's only a beam. She hands it back to me. As soon as I take hold of it, the bright, breathtaking bluebird appears—and then wreaks havoc. She circles the room, tearing down the chandelier above the overturned dining room table, knocks over the one vase that was still standing, and nearly eats Fred the spider as he sits on my knee. Just in time, I cover Fred with my free hand, and turn the flashlight off again before she can reach him.

"I don't think she just destroys bad guys," I say.

"Um, yeah," Germ says.

Under Ebb's worried gaze, I shepherd Fred into my pocket.

"This time," Germ suggests, looking thoughtful, "maybe see if you can control it more. Like, be calm, know what you want to point it at. Try to think of it as an extension of you. Like your arm or something. That's what we learned in nunchucks class." Germ has taken every athletic class known to mankind.

I warily hold the flashlight again, taking a deep breath before I turn it on, then direct it at a safe, empty corner of the room.

The little bluebird appears again. This time, though, she is slow and gentle, pecking around the floor at imaginary seeds. She seems to suddenly notice us, looks over, cocks her head inquisitively. I tense up as she hops toward me, nervous she'll hurt me. But she only hops up onto my hand.

My fingers twitch a little. She feels like part air and part feathers. Like a half-imaginary, half-material thing. She appears to like me. To want to *please me*, actually.

"We should name her," Germ says. "How about 'Chauncy'?"

"Chauncy" is Germ's name for everything that needs a name, because she thinks it's funny.

"I knew a boy named 'Chauncy,'" Ebb says wistfully. Germ snorts into her hand.

The bird sits on my finger, nuzzling up to me, chirping very softly—as if she didn't harbor a powerful, destructive side. She doesn't have much of a voice, but her liquid dark eyes hold cleverness, I decide. And courage, despite her size.

"Little One," I say decisively. "She looks like a Little One."

We walk out onto the lawn, so that we won't break anything else in the house. (Not that it matters with the house already so broken—we just don't want things to land on our heads.)

"Get her to do some stuff," Germ says.

I direct my flashlight—and Little One along with it—at a piece of paper on the grass. She pecks at it, and it bursts into small flames. I direct her up into the air, and watch her fly, quick and sure, darting in and out around trees, diving and soaring. I point her at a chair that's been tossed out of my house, and she flies right at it, takes one little peck at its leg, and the leg breaks in half.

"She's, like, a barreling bluebird of destruction," Germ says, impressed. "Do you think she'll be enough . . . if the Memory Thief comes for you?"

"I don't know," I say.

I think we're all wondering, not *if* but *when*. I hate the thought of always hiding, always waiting for the Memory Thief to appear.

"I wish we could find her first instead," I say. She *is* the only witch, it seems from what I've learned, that might be reachable somewhere in the world.

As I ruminate on this, something happens to Little

One. Fluttering up toward a tree branch, she begins to fade, and suddenly blinks out.

I shake the flashlight, but nothing happens.

And then I realize. "Batteries."

As Germ and I search the kitchen for more, I think about something the cloud shepherd said.

"A witch weapon is limited only by the boundaries of your own heart," I say to Fred in my pocket, sardonically. Your own heart, and battery life, I guess.

It takes the wind out of my sails. My weapon is a dinky little plastic flashlight that cost three dollars, and it's useless without batteries. Little One may be able to crunch on chairs and paper and moths, but a witch is a much bigger thing. What if Little One's not strong enough? She seems pretty ferocious, but she's also tiny. As much as I hate to admit it, it's still hard to think she could be any match for a witch.

I turn the flashlight beam on again once the new batteries are in. Little One appears perched on a chair, looking at me inquisitively. I walk outside again, to where Ebb is waiting, looking thoughtful.

As she flutters up toward a tree, something draws Little One's attention toward the woods. Suddenly she's executing a thrilling dive through the air—barreling across the distance faster than I've ever seen anything move. I see, just before she reaches her target, what she's going for: it's a memory moth, floating out of the edge of the woods, probably looking for me. Whatever the reason, Little One swoops down on it like a dive-bomber. Though it's almost as big as she is, she snatches it out of the air and eats it in one gulp, chomping with bright-eyed satisfaction, tilting her head this way and that as if to savor the flavor.

We wait breathlessly for a distant screech, the sound of the Memory Thief losing one of her precious creatures. But there is nothing, no sound, no anything. Maybe Homer's right, that the witch is somewhere licking her wounds. I look at Ebb and Germ, and after a few minutes of waiting, we all exchange a giddy smile.

Then Little One tilts her head, staring toward the woods again. She chirps and chirps and chirps at me.

And then she again barrels into the woods.

I see just a flash of her—soaring toward a treetop— and there's a bright flicker as she catches another memory moth in her mouth, then gently lets it go. She circles back to me, chirping, restless.

"I think she's telling you something," Ebb says.

I look at Little One, uncertain. "What?"

"Maybe you don't have to wait for the Memory Thief to come for you," Germ offers suddenly. "The moths are all sent by *her*, right, from wherever she hides?"

I nod, slow to catch on. And then it hits me.

"Little One can follow the moths," I say, breathless.

"I'll come with you," Ebb says, "as far as I possibly can."

I try to process what he's saying. It hits me hard. I feel scared, maybe even more scared than I did the night I first got the sight. Because I know what this means.

It means it's time to find the Memory Thief, and fight.

It's not easy to pack everything you need to survive a journey to find a witch, especially in a trailer full of sleeping people without waking anyone up. But my mom sleeps soundly as Germ and I move about the main room, stuffing my backpack full of granola bars, water bottles, Gatorade, nuts and peanut butter, Slim Jims, bread, and peanut M&M's.

I roll up my sleeping bag and connect it to the pack with Germ's brother's belt. I'm wearing layers: a sweater, tights, coat, hat, and scarf. I've already taken all the money out of my mom's wallet, and left a piece of paper with the letters *IOU* in its place, because I saw it in a movie once. I slip Fred the spider into my pocket, ever so slowly. He's already, in the short time we've been home, built a web in the corner of the room with the beginnings of a word.

In the bathroom, I splash warm water on my face to wake myself up. In the steam on the window, I write, *You can do this, sweetie.*

Germ lays a note for her mom on the kitchen counter, lingers for a moment staring at it, and then stands at the door, silhouetted by the porch light, waiting. It doesn't register, for the moment, why she'd do such a thing. I am too lost in thoughts of leaving, my throat aching.

I stand over my mom on the couch for a moment, looking down at her sleeping form. I crouch beside her, and think: *Either I'll succeed and see her again and the curse will be broken, or I'll never see her again at all.* Ever so gently, I touch her shoulder and give her a soft kiss on the cheek.

"I'm going to fight the Memory Thief. I'm not sure if I'll be back," I whisper. "But if I do come back, I hope you remember me then."

I step toward the door. Then I gasp. *Extra batteries. I almost forgot.*

Germ directs me to a pack in one of the kitchen drawers, and I stuff them into my bag. Then I follow her out into the yard. Ebb has promised to meet us halfway between our houses.

It's not until we are a few minutes down the trail (walking, this time—too loaded down to bike) that I realize Germ is also carrying a backpack. I halt abruptly.

"You're coming?" I say.

Germ looks slightly sheepish.

"I thought I could take you just as far as I can."

I stand there hesitating, unsure whether I should let her come or not.

"I left a note for my mom. I told her I'd be gone for a few days and I'd explain when I got back and to try not to worry. If at the end of three days, we haven't found anything, I'll turn back."

"That's six days. And worry? She's going to lose her marbles."

Germ doesn't say anything for a minute because she knows I'm right. "I brought tons of beef jerky. *Tons.*"

I still don't know. The thought of having Germ with me as I set off into the woods is about the most comforting thing I can imagine in the world right now. But I want her to stay.

"Rosie," Germ says. "I know I can't fight a witch. I know it's not my destiny like you. My destiny is to be, like, a normal person. But I still want to help. I'll come as far as I can. And then I promise, I'll let you go."

I don't know how many days or miles it will take to get to the witch. It may be that it's a distance too great to travel and that I'll have to turn back anyway. But I soften as I think, *At least I will have Germ for part of the way.*

"Okay," I relent. "But when it's the right time, you've got to let me go."

Germ nods. "I will. I promise."

Ebb is waiting for us in a patch of moonlight at a familiar boulder where I asked him to meet me. There's a light dusting of frost on the ground, and trees that make everything sparkle.

"You packed light," Germ jokes, because of course he is just floating there like he always is.

"Are you sure you want to do this?" I ask Ebb.

He nods.

"I haven't ventured more than a mile or so from home since I died," he says, "but there's a first time for everything," he says. He looks scared.

We stand for a moment, staring at each other. And then I pull my flashlight from around my neck. I point it at the horizon to the north, and Little One appears, sitting on a path of dry leaves ahead of us, tilting her head at me quizzically. I breathe deeply.

"Follow the moths," I tell her. "Just don't eat them. We don't want to draw attention to ourselves."

Little One is zipping over the trees—a flash of luminous bright blue against the dark. And then she is gone. We stand there in silence and wait. Minutes pass. We look at each other, nervous, the forest hushed.

And then there's a *woo-wup-woo-wup-woo* far off in the trees. And Little One shoots up above the treetops in the distance like a tiny firework, chasing a tiny, luminous moth. She stops midair, and then hovers. She's waiting for us to follow.

We trudge into the woods.

I glance over at Ebb, who appears pained.

"You okay?" I ask him. And he looks over at me and nods.

"Does it hurt?" Germ asks.

Ebb considers this like he isn't sure. "I feel like my soul is at the end of a yo-yo string that's stretched too far. Yeah, it hurts."

"Do you want to turn back?" I ask.

He shakes his head. "It's bearable," he says. He takes the lead before I can argue.

When we catch up with Little One, I point my flashlight forward again like a kind of command, and she takes off. She covers lots of distance, but never goes so far that we can't hear her *woo-wup-woo-wup-woo,* and see her little figure when it rises, victorious, from the trees. Each time she finds a new moth, she circles like a beacon—her bright blue shining iridescent in the dark sky.

"The moths may end up stretching all the way to Japan," Germ says.

And with that cheerful thought, we walk into the night and whatever it may hold.

CHAPTER 26

The sounds of Seaport—the occasional hum of far-off cars, the ever-present sound of the sea—fall away behind us as we walk deeper into the woods. Soon all we can hear is the rustling of leaves and the occasional but reliable *woo-wup-woo* of Little One as she finds another memory moth. Up above, the stars look as if someone has thrown a handful of bright seeds across the sky.

Occasionally we cross a road cutting its way across the forest, or pass a remote house nestled in the trees, but mostly we are on our own.

At dawn, we come to a stop, as the memory moths and Ebb and Little One—all the invisible world—disappears.

"I'll wake at my grave at dusk," Ebb says. "And get here as soon as I can." A moment later he fades and then is gone. Germ and I sleep in a patch of sun for most of the day, our sleeping bags huddled together, trying to keep warm.

At dusk we rise. Fred has crawled out of my pocket and made a web in the tree above us, with a half-finished picture of a flower. I gently reach up to where he sits and drop him back into my pocket. We eat, and wait for Little One to come to life in the beam of my flashlight and for Ebb to return.

It doesn't take long. By the time the growing sliver of moon is rising above the trees, we see his luminous form coming toward us in the dimness. He's not winded, of course, but looks more pained than yesterday. The separation from home is clearly wearing on him more tonight. We don't say much to each other as we pack up and begin again.

As we make our way along the miles in the night, and stop to eat now and then, we quickly realize that what I thought was a month's worth of jerky and peanut M&M's is not going to last that long at all. The more I think about it, the whole thing—setting off to find a witch who could be anywhere in the world—seems like a crazy idea. I think reality is sinking in for Germ, too. I'm starting to get blisters, and even Germ has been limping a little. Turns out Keds are not the best hiking shoes.

"My mom's gonna be so mad," she says glumly. "I'm sure she's called the police by now. What if they send bloodhounds after us?"

"I think that was only in the 1950s, they did that," I say, but I'm not sure.

The one bright side is that as we walk, the number of memory moths appears to be growing. Instead of flying so far ahead that she's almost beyond hearing distance, Little One is now finding the luminous moths more and more frequently and closer together as the night stretches on. It's as if they are gathering, all moving in the same direction toward some common destination. Then again, that could be wishful thinking.

But by three a.m. by Germ's watch, there are so many of them that we can follow the moths ourselves without Little One's help. They look like clusters of stars on the trees, crawling along the ground. Ebb takes to floating on ahead of us, to see if he can find out anything interesting in the near distance.

He zips back a few times, but then he doesn't come back at all.

And then the sky begins to get light. We realize we are not going to see Ebb again this night, and keep exchanging worried glances.

Finally, legs aching, feet sore, exhausted from walking more than we've ever walked in our lives—we nervously go to sleep and hope he'll come back at nightfall.

We wake well past dark. Ebb is there waiting for us, perched on a rock and staring into the distance ahead. He turns as I rustle awake, and his face is hard to read. Something has happened.

"What is it?" I ask, sitting up and rubbing my eyes, the cold outside of my sleeping bag a rude awakening. Beside me, Germ stirs too.

Ebb looks at me a long time, and then says, "I found something last night, just before I vanished."

"What?"

"Better if I just show you, I think."

We follow Ebb through the woods. At his urging, I

leave my flashlight off, so we only have the moon and the stars and moths and Ebb as light. Finally he leads us into a thick scrub of bushes and thorns. On and on we go, picking our way slowly through the dense, forbidding undergrowth, through ravines and crags filled with thorns. I wonder if maybe he's forgotten we can't float through obstacles like he can. My hands, even through my mittens, are pricked, my clothes torn.

But then, pushing prickers and scrubby bushes aside, I see that he's come to a stop—and that he's staring at something ahead of him that's hard to make sense of. It looks like a big glowing, fluttering mouth looming up from the dark ground, its lips squirming with glowing light, purple, yellow, deep pinks, blues.

A few steps closer, and I see that it's not a mouth at all—but an opening into a rocky outcropping, every inch covered in moths. It's a cave.

Moths are crawling in and out of it. It's covered in a kind of strange material, and I realize it is the gray, silky fabric of a cocoon. The silk is so thick that, if it weren't for the illumination of the memory moths, it would blend in and just appear to be more rock.

Nobody has to tell me that the Memory Thief has been here.

"But how . . . so close?" I wonder out loud. Not three nights' walk away from my house, and we're at the entrance to her hiding place? It's too much of a coincidence.

Ebb already has this figured out, however.

"She must have these entryways all over the world," he says. "Hidden where no one ever finds them. This must be how she comes and goes. I'll bet there are thousands of them, maybe tens of thousands. I bet they all lead to one place."

We stare at the cave for a long time. A slight, cool breeze emanates from inside—it smells old, a stony, musty breath of the earth.

"She's in there somewhere," I whisper.

We stand there several minutes before it really sinks in that this is a place I have to enter. And one I have to enter without Germ. Who knows how much farther and longer the journey will be once I'm inside?

I turn to look at her, and by the pained, confused expression on her face, I can see she's thinking the same thing. She opens her mouth to say something, but I say it for her.

"You can't come with me," I say.

Germ looks torn, like she thinks this is the truth but also doesn't want it to be.

"This is something I have to do. Nobody else," I say. "This is my fight, not yours."

Germ nods, but there are tears squeezing out of her eyes.

"Will you be okay to get home on your own?" I ask.

"Oh sure," she says, "definitely." But she's bluffing. I can see that a solitary, three-day hike in the woods is not exactly an easy thing to contemplate.

"Will you start back now?" I ask. She nods.

"If you need me . . . ," she says. "If you need anything at all, send Little One for me."

I nod. And then I reach my arms around her neck, hugging her hard. She squeezes me back fiercely. I don't want to let go, but finally I do.

We all stand there, waiting for someone to make a move first. And then I realize that that someone has to be me.

I take one last glance at the beautiful, full-of-life, outside world, and the sky full of stars. I look at Ebb, and he nods at me sadly. I wave good-bye to Germ, and I guess to everyone and everything else, too. And then I step across the threshold, pushing my way through the thick silk of the entrance. It gives and comes apart around me as I enter, and I brush it off me with a shiver.

Ebb puts his hand over his heart, gives a gentle smile to Germ, and then he follows me.

I turn on my flashlight and shine it down into the dark. Little One flutters ahead, though she flutters lower and slower than before, pausing here and there to perch and look around her. Even *she* looks scared and uncertain.

Together, we enter the cave and leave the world behind—only one of us with a beating heart that pounds as we move forward.

CHAPTER 27

We are in a narrow tunnel of rock stretching back into the dark, on a slight tilt downward.

Ebb at first trails along behind me, but soon he passes through me and takes the lead. He begins disappearing around curves up ahead to scout things out. Moths line the way, fluttering along the walls, but with Little One close by, they stay away from me. With each step, the air gets cooler.

I haven't been walking long when Ebb comes drifting back to me, looking at me strangely.

"What is it?"

"Well, the tunnel sort of ends up ahead."

"Ends?" I ask. This can't be the end.

"*Sort of* ends," Ebb says, but with a nervous look, full of dread.

"What do you mean, '*sort of* ends'?"

He simply turns, and I follow.

I see what he means a few moments later, when we reach a dead end with only a small hole in the rock wall ahead of us. It's just big enough for a person to fit through but not by much. It's covered in the same silky cocoon material as the cave mouth. As I shine my flashlight deeper in to take a look, my heart quickens.

"It's not a path anymore," I whisper to Ebb. "It's a slide."

"I tried floating down a bit, but I didn't get to the end. It just seems to keep going and going down. So I floated back up."

"But . . . ," I say, staring down into the darkness into which the slide plummets, "if I slide down, there's no way to get back up. Not for *me*."

This, I realize, is why Ebb looks so filled with dread. He nods solemnly.

My heart is beating so hard, it feels like it could stop as

I force myself to move the silky covering of the slide aside, and climb up—crouched—into the hole.

My fingers clutch the rock wall on either side of me to hold me still. The slide is so steep that already it's hard to keep myself from sailing down into the darkness.

"Will you go first?" I ask breathlessly. "And meet me at the bottom?"

Ebb nods.

I peer down into the silky, slippery tunnel. I remember a lake Germ's mom used to take us to as kids, and how it felt for us to jump in—those first days in late spring when the water was still so cold. How Germ would take the leap right off the bat but I would linger, scared of that first moment of being airborne, when I couldn't turn back.

"You'll be with me down there?" I ask Ebb.

"Yes," Ebb says. "I will."

"Okay," I say. I try to slow my breath, but it's coming fast. "Go ahead."

Ebb nods, floats down into the darkness, then disappears. Soon even his glow is gone.

I hold my breath, and think about my mom.

And then I let go, and slide.

At first I think I'm imagining it. Far below me in the dark as I slide, a haunting, scratchy music echoes. An old-timey voice croons,

> *"We just discovered each other*
> *Tonight when the lights were low.*
> *One dance led up to another*
> *And now I can't let you go."*

I've been sliding down and down and down for what seems like forever, my stomach lodged in my throat, my legs numb with the feeling of cresting the peak of a roller coaster. As the time has ticked by, I've steadied myself a little so I'm not slipping around so much. I've pointed my feet, with my hands at my sides to stabilize me. The slide twists and turns, it spirals, it dips so steeply at times, I almost lose contact. It feels like I'm sliding right down under the ocean, right down to the center of the earth. I try to remember if the core of the earth is hot or cold, but I can't. I shouldn't have daydreamed through geology. How far and long have I gone? Hours? Miles?

But now, the music. And—if my eyes aren't playing

tricks on me—a glimmer of something far below me. A flickering of light.

And then seconds later, with a shock, I'm truly airborne and out of the darkness, falling through nothing but empty air.

I land, and bounce, and land and bounce again.

After a few moments, I'm still enough to see what, exactly, I've landed on, but I can't quite make sense of it. I'm on the top of a huge pile of . . . old mattresses.

I stare up at the stone ceiling high above, and the hole out of which I've fallen, in a daze. With a sinking heart, I know I'll never reach that hole again. Then I look down and see that Ebb is hovering near the ground below, staring up at me, a mixture of relief and fear on his face.

"You okay?" he asks.

I nod.

I roll onto my side, and off the mattresses, tumbling down little by little till I reach the ground. The music is still playing.

> *"So tell me I may always dance*
> *The 'Anniversary Waltz' with you.*
> *Tell me this is real romance,*
> *An anniversary dream come true."*

We're in an enormous craggy underground space. There are cobwebs in the upper curves of the ceiling and memory moths fluttering around, but there are also signs that there is someone in these underground caverns besides us. The space is lit by torch-lined walls, and I see that everywhere inside the cavern there are piles and piles of *things*: books, old bicycles, video game cartridges, old clocks with broken faces. And far off along one of the craggy walls, an old record player is spinning its scratchy tune.

I crouch next to the nearest pile of books and sift through it. They're books written in languages I don't know, books of Greek mythology, coloring books, old romance novels.

"There's a path—but much bigger than the tunnel, more like a series of caverns. It just keeps spiraling down," Ebb says, his glow still very dim, his face almost sick.

"It looks like," I say, peering around, "she's really . . . nostalgic." Ebb is quiet.

"What's with the music?" I ask him.

Ebb stares hard at me, then looks over at the record player. I don't think I've ever seen him quite so worried, if that's possible.

"This was my parents' song," he says. "It was the song they played at their wedding. They used to play it for me, on their anniversary, and dance with each other."

He looks at me.

"I don't know if it's a coincidence. But maybe she knows we're here. Maybe she's toying with us."

A shiver runs through me. I wish I could reach for Ebb's hand, but the distance between the dead and the living is too big for that.

"Well," he says, glancing over his shoulder, dim and drained-looking. "We should be quiet, so that if she doesn't know we're here, she won't find out." He doesn't look so hopeful about that, though. "Shall we?"

I follow him toward the opening of the next cavern, and we move ahead.

The more we walk, the more honeycombed and vast the caverns become. Smaller tunnels branch off from our main path in all directions, and everywhere there are things stacked in corners and pathways: old paintings, and ancient carved wooden figures piled up next to used tires, stop signs, model trains, all covered in cobwebs.

"She's a pack rat," I breathe in wonder.

Yellowing photos stand propped against walls. Ancient marble statues, beautiful illustrated books, woven silks, entire sections of elaborate tile walls. In one enormous cavern we come upon a weather-beaten merry-go-round, paint chipping off the ornate carved horses. In another, a rusted tugboat looms up above us, leaning against the enormous stone walls. It's like a museum, or a big dusty closet, and beautiful in a way. Mementos of life on earth, hidden away inside of it. It doesn't feel like a dark and terrible lair; it feels more like a melancholy person's attic.

"Why would she want all these things if she hates people so much?" I wonder out loud.

Ebb shakes his head. "The same reason she wants their memories, I guess. She just wants to steal, and to desperately hold on to everything, I think."

I consider the times I've seen the Memory Thief. Her empty eyes. Her grasping hands. And I realize, Ebb is right. She's clinging to all this stuff, and I suppose to memories that don't belong to her too. Like she's trying to fill a hole that is too big to fill. Maybe all the witches are trying to fill something that's empty inside them; maybe they are all an absence of something beautiful.

Ahead, Ebb floats on, rounding a curve and disappearing from sight.

The minutes pass, and I don't see him again, and I start to worry. "Ebb?" I call, in a loud whisper. But no one replies.

And then I catch sight of him. He's come to a standstill and is looking down on something. Only when I'm standing beside him do I see what it is.

It's a canyon—enormous, seemingly bottomless—opening out in front of us. And it's full of moths. Bright, beautiful moths, pulsing with yellows, oranges, and golds. Millions of them, maybe billions of them. A multitude.

A gossamer bridge made of silk is suspended over the canyon. And out above the abyss, at the middle of the bridge and towering several stories into the sky, is an enormous cocoon.

My body swims with chills. I know, without even having to question it, that *that's* where I'll find the Memory Thief.

We stand silently, staring. I glance again down at the canyon below, full of moths and therefore full of lost history, lost love, repeated mistakes.

"So many memories," I say after a moment's shocked silence, anger pulsing from my head to my feet. "These *belonged* to people. They were never supposed to be hers. All because she's too empty to have her own."

The more I stare at all the countless memories taken, the more enraged I get. The more I hate this witch and all the other witches too.

There's something I've noticed over the years. When I'm angry, I'm especially clumsy. I bump into walls. I crash into things. It's like my negative thoughts drive me to run into the closest thing I can find.

And now is no exception. As I turn abruptly away from the canyon, in a cloud of rage, I twist off kilter on one foot and lose my balance, and then stomp against the ground to right myself. I don't mean to kick anything out of place. But there's a tiny pebble right where my shoe lands, and it goes flying out into the void below us. It clatters along a rocky outcropping as it falls downward. For a split second, Ebb and I go still, and wait.

And then the entire abyss of moths erupts with the sound of millions of wings as the horde of creatures—all at once—lifts into the air, flapping all around us. They swirl and spin for several seconds and then settle back down as quickly as they took flight. Still, the sound has been deafening.

Inside the cocoon, a light flickers on.

We gape at it, and the long narrow bridge that leads to it. I feel like I'm going to be sick.

"I think she knows we're here," Ebb says.

CHAPTER 28

We've been standing for a couple of minutes while I wait for the courage to set foot on the bridge— as if courage were some kind of package that just arrives at your door and then you have it, and then you're okay.

But I suppose courage is not just going to show up inside me all of a sudden. I guess it probably didn't work like that for my mom, either, when she crossed the world looking for witches. I guess it's more like jumping into the lake behind Germ: you just make the move. You take the step. I'm going to have to put one foot in front of the other and step onto the bridge, courage or no.

I lay my backpack down and pull out some new batteries, and replace the ones in my *Lumos* flashlight just in case. My hands are trembling as I slip the flashlight back around my neck.

Ebb stares at me, dim and mournful. I long to shake his hand, or give him a hug, but both things are impossible.

"I wish I believed I could do this," I say.

"I think you could take on a witch and then some," Ebb replies.

"Why do you think that?" I ask, wishing he could convince me, but knowing he can't.

He stands for a moment, thinking. "Because you give me hope. And that's not a little thing."

I swallow, embarrassed.

"If I don't come back, I hope you get Beyond soon."

He nods. "I know you'll be back. I'd never count you out, Rosie Oaks."

"Thanks, Ebb."

"I'll watch from here for as long as I can."

I nod. "Okay."

I take a deep breath.

I turn to the bridge.

I take the step.

My stomach dips with weightlessness as I move my feet along the narrow path perched above the canyon. I want to look back at Ebb, but I'm afraid I'll lose my balance. I'm also afraid to look down.

It's just like the path to Germ's house, sweetie, I think. *It's just as narrow as that.* But then I think of how many times I've tripped on the path to Germ's house or knocked my bike into a tree, and I try to think of something else.

I keep my eyes on the cocoon in front of me, scared that any moment the Memory Thief might come hurtling out at me, or set her moths on me. But, though the light continues to flicker in the one window, all stays still and quiet.

There's a kind of landing at the end of the bridge, spun tightly of cocoon silk. At first I think it might not hold me, but testing one foot on it, I see it's incredibly strong. I climb onto it, and look back at the canyon with relief. Far on the other side, so far away that he looks small now, Ebb lifts his hand in a wave. I wave back.

I pull my flashlight from around my neck and turn it on. There are three silken stairs that lead to a hole in the cocoon that serves as the entrance.

I climb the stairs slowly, take one last look back across the canyon at Ebb, and enter.

✦ ✦ ✦

Inside, the cocoon doesn't look like a cocoon at all, but like the interior of an old house frozen in time. There's a curving staircase with a carved railing that climbs to the floors above. There's a parlor and a dining room table, lit only by the flickering flames of a corner fireplace, black-and-white photos of random people from different eras on its mantel. There's a record player in the corner playing some old jazz number with no words. Everything—the photos, the mantel, the record player, the dining room table and chairs—is covered in cobwebs.

As I stand there taking it in, the song comes to an end and the record begins to crackle and squeak, ready to be turned over. And then I hear something else.

The sound is faint at first, but unmistakable the longer I stand there in silence. It's a *creak, creak, creak, creak* coming from the floor above me.

I clutch my flashlight and point it at the ceiling, where Little One appears, fluttering in the rafters. She flies down near me and perches on one of the cobwebbed dining room chairs, pecking at her feet where the cobwebs stick to her, perturbed. Even she looks afraid, shaking the sticky cobwebs off her beak.

I point her toward the stairs, and she flies to the bottom one, flutters above it.

Together, we make our way up.

Somewhere above, the creaking stops.

At the top I find a hallway that stretches down past a long series of rooms.

I make my way past each of them, peering inside—each full of old, homey things: toys and dressers and beds and calico curtains, web-covered, dusty. The windows—which are really just holes with no glass—are enclosed by silken strands so that it all feels shut in and claustrophobic.

I make my way to the very end of the hall and the last room. After looking side to side to make sure it's empty, I cross to the one small opening that looks down to the canyon below. This is where we saw the flickering, but now the room is only shadowy and dark. Ebb must have left, because I can't see him where I left him at the edge of the bridge.

And then I hear it.

Creak, creak, creak. Right behind me.

I turn and see what I missed—tucked just to the side of the open door and obscured by it.

A rocking chair. And a woman sitting in it.

She's covered in cobwebs too, and is so still, she looks

almost petrified. Her face is neither young nor old, beautiful nor haggard. She is all in purple, and she looks—not terrifying like she did the last time I saw her, when she was reaching out to curse me, but—lost. On her lap is a blanket covering some shape I can't make out. There's pain on her face, and her fingers are grasping, grasping at the air as if plucking at invisible mosquitoes.

"You've come to take something from me," the Memory Thief says.

Little One, who's been fluttering about the room, alights on my shoulder and perches there making a *click, click, click* sound with her beak—either for fear or warning.

I try to take courage from the fact that she's with me, but she's agitated like me.

"I only want what belongs to my mother," I say.

The Memory Thief frowns softly, and looks down at her lap. She pulls the blanket aside. As she does, chills swim up and down my arms, because there in her gnarled hands is a metal cage. And in the cage are hundreds of tiny purple and blue and yellow and pink and orange moths. I know in my bones what they are.

My mother's memories.

"I've been looking them over for the first time," the Memory Thief says, "all these memories. I steal so many—

millions, billions—even the interesting people are hard
to get around to. Though I *should* have looked, I suppose.
I would have known about *you* even before you had the
sight." She sighs, low and deep. "These ones are lovely.
There is so much love, so much courage. Your birthdays,
your milestones—they're here too." She waves to the air,
indicating the world at large. "I may not ever get to see
even a fraction of the memories I've collected, but every
single one is precious to me. I'm afraid I can't give these
ones back to you."

She looks so fragile, sad and wounded. Not the vicious
witch I've been so afraid of meeting.

"You've come a long way with your little friend." The
Memory Thief nods to Little One. "But you've been very
foolish. It's not for children to defeat witches, no matter
what the storybooks say. And it's not for sweet little bird-
ies, either." The Memory Thief stands, frowning at me. "I
know how it is. You want to hold so tight to the things you
love, never let them go. But only *I* can truly hold on to the
past, Rosie. Not you."

I start to feel a prick of panic. Because I'm realizing
quickly, she's not afraid that I've found her, and not afraid
of Little One. As frail as the Memory Thief appears, she
does not seem frightened at all.

Unintentionally, her eyes dart toward the ground. It's the only warning I get. I look down and let out a cry.

Moths have crawled into the room, thousands of them. They cover the floor and, though I haven't noticed them, are all over my legs.

I stumble backward with a cry. I grasp my flashlight and shine it down at my legs.

Little One dives, but is instantly swarmed by moths. They're on her so fast and thick that her wings flap only once before she tumbles onto the ground. She flaps madly, tries to lift off again, but they're clinging to her back, her beak, her tail.

And then I feel a cold hand grip my arm, and I turn as my flashlight is pulled out of my grasp. The Memory Thief darts backward, my flashlight in her hands. And just like that, she reaches the one small window, extends her arm, and drops my flashlight out.

I watch in horror as Little One, in her struggle with the moths, flickers a few times and then disappears completely. A cacophony rises from below, thousands of moths rising from the canyon into the air.

I turn my eyes to the cage of my mother's memories, lying on its side near the rocking chair. I lunge for it, but the Memory Thief is there in a moment, blocking my way, shaking her head. She latches one gnarled hand on to my arm, and her grip is like steel—nothing like the touch of the frail woman she appears to be.

"It looks like you've come all this way, dear, to be disappointed. Witches can't be killed. You must have been told that, and still you've come. You were right when you burned your stories that night. Oh yes, I know about that. There is no magic in the world to speak of. Not the kind you hoped for, at least."

She holds her free hand out above the floor, and the moths begin to rise. They start to land on me, though I try to knock them away. But I'm covered, drowning in dusty shimmering wings.

It happens so fast. The witch's fingers send a feeling like ice through my arm as she curses me. My memories begin to leave me, not in a trickle but in a wave. I observe them as they go:

My mom, sitting at the window, saying, "He's out there swimming, waiting for me."

My mom as a girl in a cloud shepherd's misty hands.

My mom and my dad in the photo in the attic, looking at each other with so much love.

Watching D'quan Daniels eat a dirt sandwich in the second grade.

Telling a story to Germ on the phone to help her sleep.

Germ and me racing in the yard.

Germ on the first day of kindergarten, huddled at the foot of the door.

Germ wearing eyeliner for the first time.

Ebb and me sitting on the cliff and watching the sea.

Homer Honeycutt saying, "Only the witches would have you think there is more darkness in the world than there is light."

So many memories, all beginning to blur and fade away. I feel tears running down my cheeks as I watch these visions turn to iridescent dust and fall through the air, gathered on the wings of the moths that flutter all around me.

And then I can't remember why I'm crying.

And then I feel myself lifted by the moths, carried through the halls of the cocoon as if on a moving, fluttering bed.

And then I forget to notice anything at all.

CHAPTER 29

I wake in the dark, in a round cave with no door. There is just the tiniest flicker of dim light coming from a small hole in the stone ceiling far above me.

I sit up slowly, trying to remember. Why am I here? Have I been here before? Can I walk? Can I stand? I remember vaguely the faces of a blond freckled girl and a dead boy and a woman who sits by an attic window watching the sea, but not what they mean to me or why they are in my head.

I only remember that I'm trapped and that there's no escape and that I'm small. And I remember the witch. Memories of the witch are still in my head.

I don't know how long I've slept. It could be hours or days. My stomach feels empty, but I don't remember if it's ever felt this empty before.

I stare at the wall in front of me, lit just barely by flickering light from the hole above. Then I fall back asleep.

For who knows how long, I wake and fall back asleep. My dreams are vague and shapeless and they seem to stretch on for years.

I wonder if you can disappear just by wanting to—just by sheer lack of wanting to *be*.

I roll onto my back, and close my eyes again, but just as my eyelids flutter shut, I catch a glimmer of something, and open them again.

In the faint glow from the hole at the top of the cave, I see them. In the crags and corners of the cave, in the little nooks here and there.

I think I'm imagining them at first, because they are words floating in the air on nothing, and that makes no sense.

But as my eyes adjust again to the flicker-light, I see that the words are not floating on nothing. They are woven into the thin crisscrossing silk of webs—just barely visible in the gossamer threads:

> *I am responsible for my rose.*

> *The moment you doubt whether you can fly, you cease forever to be able to do it.*

> *Hoping is such hard work.*

> *Look at how a single candle can both defy and define the darkness.*

I stand slowly, on shaky legs. The words are so familiar, even though I don't remember them. I think they are from stories.

They're woven all around me, hundreds of them. And then I see their creator—a tiny, ghostly spider working steadily in a corner of the room. He is putting the finishing touches on another one.

> *Nevertheless, as they climbed higher and higher, London unfurling below them like a*

gray-and-green map, Harry's overwhelming
feeling was of gratitude for an escape that had
seemed impossible.

I don't understand it, but one moment there's such a hollow place inside me, and the next moment the words are filling that place up. Something inside that was empty and lost a moment before feels *un-lost*. It's like the words remember something for me that I can't, and give something to me I can't find by myself. The words build something out of nothing. They put something beautiful and strong inside my chest, and the beautiful and strong thing starts to overflow into imagining.

I imagine rescues against all odds and lights in the darkness. I imagine help is coming even if everything is broken and all hope is lost.

I imagine that stone walls can't hold me. I imagine that I am the one who makes the rules, and that I am bigger and stronger than I think, unbound and unstoppable. I imagine that with nothing to lose, there is also nothing to hold me back. I call help to me, believing I can.

And then I hear a tiny . . . the tiniest . . . of sounds.

A small shape comes fluttering through the hole of the

cave. A luminous bluebird whose name, it suddenly occurs to me, is "Little One." And though she's too small for it, she's carrying a flashlight in her mouth.

"Little One," I whisper to her as she lands on my finger. She drops the flashlight into my hand. "I don't remember what to do."

Little One flutters out of my hand and around the webs above, waiting.

I read some of the words again.

Harry's overwhelming feeling was of gratitude for an escape that had seemed impossible.

I take courage.

"Little One," I say, pointing my flashlight at the floor so that she perches there, looking at me expectantly. "We can fly," I say, with only the overflowing hope that the words can be true.

Little One chirps as if excited, as if she's been waiting all along for this.

And then, she does something I don't expect. She begins to grow.

She grows and grows and grows, so big and bright and blue that the cave starts to feel small. It's getting tighter and tighter inside the cave, and I hurry over to slip the spinning spider into my pocket.

And then there is a deafening crash and rocks begin to crumble around us. Little One has outgrown the cave, and burst its walls.

In another moment, we are standing in open air— the canyon walls towering impossibly high above and all around us.

Little One looks down at me with enormous glittering black eyes as big as I am, and then she lowers one wing. I climb onto her back.

And we fly, fueled only by wishing and words.

I'm clinging tight and we're barreling up, up, and up. I don't remember where we need to go, but Little One does. And then, up above us, and getting closer fast, is an enormous cocoon.

A dark figure comes crashing out of the entrance and onto the landing, throwing her arms into the air as she sees us. We do not slow down.

She runs out onto the bridge across the abyss, letting out a horrible screech. Thousands of moths rise from all around us. But we are too fast, too big, too enraged.

Just as the figure reaches the middle of the bridge, we dive. I only know what Little One will do a moment before she does it.

She soars at the witch, opens her beak, and devours her.

With a scream cut short, and a cage of moths busting open as it flies out of her hands, the witch disappears into the bird's gaping beak.

And is gone.

I watch the moths fly out of the cage, and flutter upward. They are not the only ones.

If the moths of the canyon were loud a moment ago, they are chaos now. They flap so loudly, hitting the walls, that it feels as if my ears will break. It's a hurricane of them, so many, I can barely see anything else. The walls of the cavern begin to give off a low moan.

Walls begin to crumble all around us.

And moths begin to land on me, but I'm not afraid. Because these moths are familiar to me—or at least, their whispers are. And as they crawl and whisper over me, I begin to remember.

Little One is searching, searching for something, along the walls and tunnels that are coming apart.

And then I see a small luminous figure hovering and staring up at us. Little One swoops a wing at him, and brushes him onto her back beside me. And again, we fly up, up, up.

As the cavern bursts open, we soar into the open air.

The moths—millions of them—go with us. They flee in all directions, filling the dark sky. I watch them in disbelief.

"What are they doing?" I ask.

And the ghost boy (his name is Ebb, I remember; things are coming back fast) says, "I think they're going home."

I look upward again.

Have we set them all free? Could something that wonderful really be possible?

Flying through the air toward home, we soon see a small figure below us, a blond and freckled girl walking home through an enormous forest. She has a long way to go.

Little One dips. She takes Germ gently into one claw, and lifts her up, and soars.

CHAPTER 30

We land in my backyard, on the beach at the bottom of the cliffs. It's almost dawn.

Little One bends a wing so that Germ, Ebb, and I can slide onto the grass, and then she straightens up again.

"Thank you, Little One," I say, and turn off the flashlight, and she disappears. I know that no matter what, I'll be able to call her back when I need her.

Germ and I hug each other. Ebb swirls around in a circle, extra bright.

"Tell me everything," Germ says.

So we tell her all that happened after we left her: the tunnels of the cave, and the hoarded old things, the canyon full of moths, the cocoon, and the witch. And then, when I get to the dark room and my lost memories, I pull Fred out of my pocket and slip him onto Ebb's hand, and tell them both the rest. How Fred's words filled my empty places. How they made me imagine things I thought were impossible.

All the way home, moths have been returning memories to me. It feels almost like the memories never left. I suppose the same thing is happening to people all over the world—as the escaped moths spread out across the sky and around the globe. At least, that's what I hope. I hope that lots of people are still there to receive the memories that were taken from them.

Ebb looks down at Fred in his hand, petting him gently on his head, then slips him onto his shoulder. The sun is rising, and they have to go.

"I knew you could do it, Rosie," Ebb says. And then he begins to flicker.

In another moment, he's gone.

Germ and I watch just the slightest hint of the sky lightening as the clouds of distant moths streak out toward the horizon.

The enormity of what I've done begins to sink in.

What forgotten things are going to be remembered? Will it ever, in the smallest way, change the world? All because of a story and one tiny little imaginary bird?

Germ, who's been grinning from ear to ear, finally grows serious.

"Well, I've really got to get home. I've been living on M&M's for the past twelve hours. And my mom . . ." She looks sorrowful and deeply guilty. "I may be grounded for, like, life. But when I'm allowed, I'll call you."

"What will you tell her?"

"I'll tell her I was sleepwalking," she says, and winks. And then she gets serious again. "No, I'll tell her the truth. And she won't believe me. And she'll probably put me in therapy or something. But at least *I'll* know it's the truth. And I'll keep trying to convince her, somehow.

"Rosie . . ." She hesitates. "I was thinking about it all the time I was walking home, and I'm pretty sure I've figured it out. I think the reason I got the sight is because I love you, just like how it happened with your mom and dad, how loving her so much helped him to see what *she* saw. I think maybe loving a friend can help someone see what they see too."

She hugs me again; then we pull back and look at each other. There is still that uncertainty between us, that little bit of distance. But we are too happy to be bothered by it now. And I think maybe she is right about the sight, and how she got it.

"I'll walk you up to the driveway," I say.

We are just stepping onto the steep trail up to the yard when I hear it.

I put a hand on Germ's arm.

She turns to me with a quizzical look.

"What?" she asks, but I hold a finger in front of my mouth, and listen hard.

It's an unfamiliar sound, coming from the direction of the cliffs. I know what the sound is, but it makes no sense. It's hard to distinguish above the wind off the sea. But I have a prickling, itching feeling.

"It sounds like someone calling my name," I say.

Germ tilts her head and then nods. "I hear it too."

It's definitely coming from up on top of the cliffs now. Someone is calling, calling me.

We make our way up the path as fast as we can. Just as we crest the ridge, I see her walking along the cliff's edge, her long dark hair blowing in the breeze. She's staring in the opposite direction, searching for something.

"Rosie!" she's calling. "Rosie!" Out of breath, as if her life depended on finding me. She's so disheveled and upset, it looks as if she's run all the way here.

"I'm here!" I call to my mom, and she whips around to see me.

She clutches her hands to her chest. Her eyes fill with tears.

"Rosie?" she yells, her shoulders sinking in relief—the way you feel when you find something you've lost that you care about more than anything else in the world. She smiles so big, the way you might smile if someone gave you an island in Hawaii, I guess.

"Where have you been?" she calls to me.

And then she opens her arms, and I rush into them.

PART 3

CHAPTER 31

Here's a thing or two I've learned about memories.

They are like seeds; love can grow from them. They look different depending on the day when they are remembered. They are slippery, malleable things, apt to be altered. They can be clutched too tightly. Their absence can cause fractures that run deep between people, towns, whole countries. They are meant, sometimes, to be let go. And yet, the night the Memory Thief was destroyed and the memory moths set free, the world became a little better for it.

Everywhere, strange, subtle things have happened—stories I see on the news: Grandparents who've forgotten names and faces suddenly smiling at their grandchildren. Amnesiacs showing up in their families' backyards. Towns publicly reflecting on histories long forgotten. Even if people don't see the invisible moths in the sky, dropping dust on them like snow, maybe they feel it.

Even the reporters look happy as they relate these stories.

Like memory, time is both a measurable thing and an immeasurable one. It's true that at the end of our curling and lonely road in Maine, the months pass. It's also true that, under the surface of the sea, time stays in one place, or rather a million places at once. And I think about it all the time. I think about *them*. The witches.

Are they coming for me? Are they scared of me? Do they know who or where I am? Do they know what I did? The days pass, and there are no answers, and I settle into a fragile kind of safety. The longer it lasts, the less likely it seems they will ever arrive. Maybe the idea that a witch hunting weapon has succeeded again, after all these years, is enough to keep them away forever. Homer did call them cowardly creatures. I count on it now.

It takes my mom time to remember everything, and some of the years are still foggy. The days before I was born are vivid to her—her time hunting witches, meeting my dad, hiding her books, that terrible night at the hospital—but the years since then are hazy. What's not hazy is how much she loves me.

I am getting to see who she really is, and coming to know the person who once filled my room with wonder and colors and powerful words. That person has exploded into my world, and I see why the witches feared her.

She is curious. She listens much harder than she speaks and plows through books and newspaper articles, soaking up things like a sponge.

She is angry in a way that makes me feel strong.

"Nobody's doing anything about the polar bears?" she demands, the edge of a fight in her voice. "We'll see about that, Rosie," she adds, as if she thinks anything can be fixed if you just have the right strategy. She has that "We'll see about that" tone in her voice about a lot of things—a mixture of rage and purpose. Her voice is colorful and lively at these moments—like gravel and roses. (At other times, when she's just talking with me about nothing at all, it lilts like a feather in a breeze.)

She is efficient—not one for moping over what she's lost. One of the first things she does is tackle my room: organizing my books, replacing all the notes I've put on the walls with notes of her own:

You are a magnificent creature.
You are a miracle.
You are funny, you are smart, you are brave.

She is tireless, and when she's not tending to me, or reading, or working, she's creating. Painting everything she can see—the sea, the trees, *me*. Only, she doesn't just paint what's *there*—she captures something elusive: the hopefulness of a tree, the mystery of the ocean and what is lost in it, the sadness in my eyes when I think about my brother. She says that—like poetry and stories—art is a way of looking for something true. "A great man once said, 'An artist is here to disturb the peace.' That means an artist makes people think twice about what they don't think about hard enough."

She is hard to look away from—with cleverness and interest in her eyes.

But she is also, oftentimes, lost. She spends many days in and out of a fog, fearful and weak. "Life can sometimes break something inside you," she says, "and sometimes you can't fix it." By "life," she means what happened to my brother.

We almost never talk about Wolf (which is what we've decided to name him, since he never had a name). Those times when he comes up, a heavy helplessness settles over her. It's like the memory is too painful to fully hold in her mind. She starts to drift away, and I have to pull her back with talk of other things. I think, more than anything, it's that she doesn't know what to do to make it better. The few times she's tried her arrows, they've done nothing at all. Her witch hunting days, her longing for the thing that waited in the water for her, are over—that much is easy to see. Some things can't be fixed. And to be honest, I'm often relieved. I just want her safe.

It turns out insurance is a boring but useful thing. While we are squeezed in with the overcrowded but always cheerful Bartleys, our house is slowly rebuilt. When it's finally finished, we move back in, and the ghosts trickle back. Mom can see them now, and she and Soggy catch up on old, new, and mutual friends. He cries on her shoulder about Crafty Agatha. She has a knack for comforting ghosts. She tries to make the afterlife brighter for him and the others with jokes and compliments and music on the record player, and soon our house is full of all the neighborhood spirits (they're ghosts, so of course word travels fast)—dancing in the parlor, laughing in the kitchen, swirling up and down the stairs.

Germ likes to join us sometimes, but not as much as she used to. Sometimes she's at Bibi's house, or sometimes at D'quan's. Sometimes I am too. I'm not trying to hold on to her when I go with her. I'm just trying to see if maybe people change, even me. I'm trying to take down my walls. And the more I do, the easier it becomes. I'm even beginning to think—though I don't like to admit it to myself— that Bibi seems actually kind of okay as a person. Maybe she's even nice, I don't know.

Things with Germ and me may never be exactly what they used to be, and sometimes I worry about that. But I also try to trust that the changes are good, too. After all, I can't get back what's already gone.

Still, I know something gnaws at Germ—I can see it, just like time gnaws at *me*. She likes to flip through the newspapers and clip out the upbeat stories, then tape them to the wall in her room. With bad news, she bites her lip. She thinks and thinks, like she is figuring something out.

It's a problem, this knowing we have more power than we thought we did. Even for a non-witch-hunting, boy-crazy, longing-to-be-normal person like Germ.

Mom and I like to sit on the grass in the afternoons watching the late spring flowers bloom, basking in the sun, and taking in the breeze from the ocean. And at times like those I know we're thinking of Wolf, and how it doesn't seem right to be here without him.

Sometimes we laugh and talk, and sometimes we're quiet thinking about Wolf, and I find myself staring at the ocean. I'm happy, but I'm troubled all the time. To never really know what happened to him—it keeps me up at night, and makes my stomach ache. He might be out there, and he might not. He might be forever gone, but then, he might not.

We talk about the witches and all the things my mom has learned. There are no surprises, but there's one thing she is very careful not to mention—the thing the cloud shepherd showed me that night, that clearly she doesn't want me to know.

She only hints at it once, as we walk across the grass on our way inside one afternoon. "If you ever plan to leave me, Rosie, please don't tell me. I don't think I could stand it if you do, and I know I could never let you go." I listen for a moment in confusion. I think I understand, but I'm not sure. And I don't bring it up again.

The days go on this way: small victories, slow recoveries, sometimes giddy happiness, and sometimes deep regret and worry about what we've lost. But I'm restless. And every night, I watch the moon rise, and wonder. And every night Ebb floats around the yard keeping watch, especially on dark moons. We never know when one of the other witches might come for us, or if—as we hope—they've forgotten us altogether and moved on to things bigger than a small girl and her imaginary bluebird.

And then one dark night, when Germ is sleeping over in her sleeping bag on the floor, and the rest of the house is asleep, I wake to the sound of something in my room, or rather, the sound of nothing. It's completely silent. Germ's usual snoring has stopped.

And then I realize, with a sick feeling, what else is different. The old clock in the corner of the room has stopped. I climb out of bed and look at Germ's watch on her wrist; it's stopped too.

A moment later I see the shadow, sitting in the corner, hummingbirds whirring in the air around her.

Her powder-blue eyes stare at me in the dark.

She smiles at me with razor-sharp teeth, and eyes as empty as the eyes of a fish.

I shrink back into the corner of the room. I look at my flashlight across the room on my nightstand, but I don't dare move.

"Shhh," the Time Witch whispers. "Don't wake your mother. She's so harmless, I'd rather let her be for now." She gazes at me a long moment. "Did you think I didn't know? That I wouldn't know where to find you? Did you think I'd forgotten that you've killed my friend?"

I'm silent. I am petrified and frozen.

She seems to rethink her words. "We witches . . . we don't exactly have friends. Still, it angers me. Who are you to kill a witch?" Her teeth glint in the darkness as she smiles at me again. "No, Rosie Oaks, I haven't forgotten you. I've watched you. I've learned. I know what power you have, and what powers you don't.

"Oh, that reminds me. I brought something for you." She lays a tiny paper square on the table next to her chair, and beside it, a tiny hourglass. She looks at my flashlight in the corner. "You're welcome to bring your toy, too. It's nothing either way to me. Consider this my gift, to make up for your friend, the ghost. Turns out he's not very good at keeping watch after all."

It's as if a rock has thudded into my chest. I look toward the window for Ebb outside it. I already know I'm not going to see him.

"What did you do to him?" I whisper suddenly, in a panic. My stomach flops over sickly.

The Time Witch smiles.

"He did try to fight . . . poor, helpless thing. Seems to have a bit of a vendetta against me."

Seems, I think frantically, not "seemed." Not past tense. He might still be okay. It's a tiny detail and an uncertain one. But I cling to it.

"Perhaps you've heard that I'm quite fond of games. Things get boring when the world is at your mercy." She grins. "Well, I've got a game for you. The game is, if you want him, come and get him."

"Come for Ebb?" I whisper, but she only smiles as if at some private joke.

"Of course, you'll have to go through *them* to get to *me*. I think you may have heard that there are twelve of us left. Well, *eleven* now."

She shifts in her chair, looking out at the dark, a hummingbird darting behind her and hovering above her shoulder. The clouds are still covering the half-moon, but the breeze is blowing them. "Well, I'd better be going," the witch says, though she makes no move to leave.

"Maybe I'll see you again sometime. It would be . . . interesting. I long to be interested in something. There's nothing new under the sun these days, it seems to me. But maybe you could prove me wrong."

And then she lazily waves a hand, and the hummingbird at her shoulder darts toward me, circling me. I blink, batting it away, and when I open my eyes, the clock has jumped forward a minute or two and ticked back to life. The witch is gone.

Germ starts snoring again.

And I'm left standing in the corner of the room, watching the spot she occupied a moment before. After a second's hesitation, I make my way to the table by the chair. I pick up the tiny square of paper she left, and squint at it in the dark, then turn on my flashlight to study it further.

It's a wrinkled photo of someone I don't know, who must have lived a couple hundred years ago or more. A boy my age in an old-timey hat. The photo has got that brown tint of very old images, the kind from the Wild West and Victorian parlors, and it's marked on the bottom: *San Francisco, 1855*. The boy is small like me, brown-haired like me. He looks vulnerable, and scared, like whatever he is looking at beyond the camera scares him to death.

And my legs go weak as I realize who he is. And who the witch wants me to come for.

My brother. Alive. Or at least, he was alive when this picture was taken.

I turn it over, and on the back, in a scrawled hand, it says, *You have one month.*

I look outside at the dark grass, the dark sky.

And then I pull on my robe and slip silently out of the room. I know what I need to do.

I tiptoe out into the backyard, and walk all the way down the ocean-side trail to where the half-moon rises above the rocky outcrop of the far cliffs. There I find the bottom of the ladder dangling, an arm's length out over the sea, as if waiting just for me. At least, I have to hope that's true. If it's not . . .

I look up toward the moon and take a deep, ragged breath. I make my mind go blank to forget my fear. I reach for the ladder, grab tight, and—with a small, breathless jump—I begin to climb.

Don't disappear, I think with every breath. *Please don't disappear.*

Several minutes have passed before I even think to look down, and when I do, I grip the rungs of the ladder in terror. I see my house already tiny below. I decide not to look down again, and I keep pushing onward, getting more and more out of breath, my arms sore.

But there is also something dreamlike about the climb. I'm already much farther up than I should be. It's impossible to climb the distance before me, and yet with each rung I get noticeably farther from the land below. Up this high, the air should be cold and thin, but I feel warm and my lungs are full. My legs shake with exertion and fear, but the ladder does not disappear.

After a while, I can see the entire coast of Maine, then the shape of North America, far beneath me. There's no sign of cloud shepherds except very far in the distance and already below me.

I keep going up, up, up into the dark night just beneath the stars.

The moon looms bigger and brighter above me with every step, its light welcoming me. Soon I'm close enough to touch it. And then—impossibly, unbelievably—I'm there. I step down onto the moon's surface, all aglow.

Before me, the Moon Goddess is sitting on a chair—a throne, of sorts, but a modest one. She has long curly silver hair and silver skin and eyes that seem to stare right into me.

"You came," she says. Her voice is a whisper, yet so powerful and confident, I think I could hear it from a million miles away. I have a feeling that whatever I answer the Moon Goddess, it will be something she already knows.

"I know what was waiting for my mom in the water," I say.

"Yes," she whispers, "you do."

"And I think now, it's still waiting. But for me." The Moon Goddess watches me silently. "I don't want to go. I want to be safe and hidden and small. But my brother is out there somewhere, and I think so is Ebb. And the witches are out there somewhere too. And all the terrible things are out there somewhere. And I might be the only one who can help with any of it."

"Yes."

"And there are eleven of them. And all I have are a flashlight and some stories."

"A story can have more sway over the world than an evil man," she says simply, as if I should already know it. "It can touch more lives, change more hearts, build more courage than a dark force. The witches tell a story of emptiness and malice and mistrust and hate. You could tell the opposite story."

She pauses, and I don't speak. "You've suffered, Rosie. Would you like me to erase what you know?" she asks kindly, gently. "Would you like to forget the hidden fabric . . . me . . . your power . . . your brother? I could make you and your mother forget. Sometimes it's easier to forget what we are responsible for and what we are supposed to do. Remembering means choosing," she says.

I think about the magic and the witches and all the scary and beautiful things. How things were easier before I knew, but also harder. And I think that to wait for others to fight is not enough.

I shake my head.

I know that despite everything I want that's different, and all the weeks I've pretended that I haven't, I've already made my choice about whether I'm really a witch hunter or not.

CHAPTER 32

That night, while Germ sleeps on the floor, I climb down from the moon and tiptoe into my room, and pull a small engraved whistle from inside my pillowcase where I've been hiding it, and slip it and the small hourglass into my pocket. I tuck *The Witch Hunter's Guide* into my backpack, knowing too well the terrors it contains: the Greedy Man, Hypocriffa, the Griever, Babble, Miss Rage, Chaos, Convenia, Mable the Mad, and more: witches with murder in their eyes and weapons to curse me.

Downstairs, after filling my backpack with a few sweaters and some food and my *Lumos* flashlight, I stare out the window at the night. The trees sway in the breeze.

I try to take heart.

There's being comfortable, and then there's being brave.

I write a note for my mom—saying that I'm doing it the way she wanted, that I'm not telling her before I go.

I open her door and look at her sleeping. "Please forgive me," I whisper. Passing my door again, I peer in at Germ snoring for a moment, then keep walking, trying to step around the creaks.

Down at the beach, I almost lose my nerve. I listen to the familiar sounds of the waves on the beach and the other sounds of home, and wonder when or if I'll ever hear them again. I hold my whistle to my lips, but before I blow, a noise behind me startles me.

Standing on the sand by the bottom of the cliffs, silhouetted by the moon, is Germ. She has her sleeping bag hastily rolled under one arm and wild just-woken-up hair. She's waiting for an explanation, but it's also as if—at least partly—she already knows. She knows I'm leaving.

"It's true, the legends," I say quietly. "The whale, the sea, time. All of it." I hold up the photo of my brother.

Germ blinks at it, trying to shake off sleep. She looks at the whistle in my hands, and her eyes ask a question.

There are so many answers: Wolf, and Ebb (I hope), and the Time Witch. But they all boil down to one.

"I'm going after them," I say to her, simply.

Germ is silent for a moment, and her eyes focus.

"Me too," she says.

I shake my head, but Germ flicks her wild hair back in annoyance, and tightens her arms around her sleeping bag.

"It's my world too, Rosie," she says, "even if I'm not an Oaks. And I want to fix it."

I think of Germ obsessing over the news, the broken things in the world, and the knowledge that has gnawed at both of us: the chance we can't forget we have. I know I'm not the only one who's been trying to choose between doing nothing and doing *something*. I can't think Germ choosing *this* is also her choosing *me*. Still, my heart flutters with warmth.

"There are ten of them plus the Time Witch," I say. "And I mean to get through all of them."

"Let's get through all of them," Germ says, her mouth closing tight. Her freckles glow brighter with her anger.

I can't help it. I break into a smile.

We look at each other for a few moments nervously, and then I turn to the water and blow the whistle as hard as I can. And though the sound seems to drown in the wind, an answer comes at once. A stream of spouted water blows high into the air, making us stumble back on our feet.

And then comes the rise of a shape—like a hill suddenly emerging from the sea. Getting closer and closer, an enormous tail flaps against the waves—powerful and strong. We wade out to our knees, scared and excited, holding hands as the shape rises before us.

The whale stares at us with ancient eyes. It opens its enormous mouth.

I gasp. Inside his mouth is a small cozy room with a rug and chairs and two beds and a few warm blankets. It's not the kind of thing you'd expect inside any kind of mouth, anywhere.

"I thought I'd seen it all," Germ breathes.

"I think we're just getting started," I say.

We cast one last look at the bluff where my house stands. The trees and grass blow in the breeze—as if the trees are talking even to those of us who don't know how to listen, and the whole yard is waving good-bye.

We step inside. And the whale closes its mouth as it dives into the sea . . . and into the past.

And the witch hunt begins.

ACKNOWLEDGMENTS

Thank you to my editor, Liesa Abrams, and my agent, Rosemary Stimola, for their talent, time, and most of all, their deeply precious presence in my life. Thank you to Dannie Festa for making me feel like I have the best team in the world. Thank you to Ani Kazarian and Alison Turner for our time writing in the woods; Mara Anastas for infinite patience; Tammy Coron for showing me a better way to do things; Sarah McCabe for a fresh perspective; Chelsea Morgan, Bara MacNeill, Alison Velea, and Jen Strada for letting nothing slip through the cracks; and Heather Palisi, Jessica Handelman, and Kirbi Fagan for a beautiful cover. I want to acknowledge my husband, Mark, for carrying me through draft after draft of this story with his feedback, time, support, and love; and Monica, Lauren, Haviva, Lily, and Rebecca for allowing me to devote time to my work by caring for my babies. Much gratitude to Natalie and David for sharing their cabin in the woods!

I want to thank my mom for giving me a love of reading and my dad for always being my rock during storms.

ACKNOWLEDGMENTS

And finally, I am deeply indebted to the teachers and librarians and booksellers who make writing books possible for me and who nurture young people as passionate readers. They are some of the most powerful witch hunters in this world.

TURN THE PAGE
FOR A LOOK AT

Thirteen Witches,
BOOK 2:

PROLOGUE

*I*n the middle of the night, in a house at the end of Waterside Road, two women sit by a window looking out at the sea. They lean toward each other in their chairs as if closeness will protect them from something they fear. Outside, the frigid wind blows at the glass. It is dark moon, and Annabelle Oaks has an uneasy feeling that something is coming.

On her left, Elaine Bartley is wearing a sweatshirt that says I Could Be Wrong but Probably Not *in faded puffed letters. She's flipping through the pages of a mystery novel but barely reading it. Annabelle is elegant in a tiered cotton dress,* and smudged with paint as she stares at a canvas she is dabbing at with a brush.

They're unlikely companions, and yet the months since their daughters left have brought them together evening after evening, in this ritual of watching and waiting. On a table between them, a piece of paper lies open. It's never far from Annabelle even when she sleeps. It's the note their daughters left behind the night they went away:

I'm going to find him, *it reads. And then, below that, in a postscript scribbled crookedly at the bottom:*

I'm going too.

The first sentence is neat and steady, as if the few words it contains were measured out carefully by its author. The second sentence is sloped and wild, as if one girl were catching up to the other on her way out the door . . . as if it were written at a sprint.

This is the note the women showed the police—who believe the girls have run away to track down lost fathers they will never find. Annabelle, of course, knows better.

A sailor in a yellow rain slicker drifts into the room and then right through Elaine, to get to the kitchen. Elaine sits up taller, shivering.

"That's Soggy that went through you," Annabelle says. "Sorry. He's really quite distracted since losing Crafty Agatha."

Mrs. Bartley shivers again, looking around, then turns back to her book. She doesn't have the sight; she can't see the ghosts milling about the room, but she does sense the cold of them. The room, which would look empty to almost anyone, is actually full of spirits. More and more have come every day since Rosie left, ghosts from nearby towns and counties trying to get a glance at the Oaks family home before drifting back to their graves by morning. The death of the Memory Thief has made this house more infamous than it already was.

Annabelle knows that her companion believes her about all of it: the ghosts, the witches, the Moon Goddess, the war. She knows it's easier to believe in impossible things than to believe that someone you love is truly lost; better to think your daughter is off on a dangerous journey she chose than to believe the alternative. But Annabelle knows, also, that Elaine does not know enough of witches to fear them as she should.

Finally Annabelle's visitor stands up. "Heading home," she says, laying a gentle hand on Annabelle's shoulder before turning and shuffling toward the door. Most nights, she's here until she can barely keep her eyes open. And then she returns with circles under her eyes the next evening.

After she goes, Annabelle turns back to her painting, smudging and dotting the canvas with her brushstrokes, rendering a portrait of her grandmother. As with all her other work, there is something foreboding about it. The things Annabelle renders can't help but take a dark turn: flowers wilt in their vases, faces frown, storms whip forests of trees. There is a warning in her grandmother's eyes.

"They're out there swimming, waiting for me," Annabelle says to no one—to the painting, to the ghosts, the walls, the air, the stars.

In her mind she sees her children: Rosie, short, quirky, strong, and brave; and Wolf, a baby boy she only knew for moments before she was robbed of him. She aches with the memory—now returned to her—of the two of them on the day they were born. The tight, trusting grip of Wolf's tiny hand, the sweet smell of the top of his head, the wide wonder in his eyes looking out at the world. Rosie weeping after he was taken away that morning, reaching for him as if she'd lost her own arms.

One child stolen. The other now grown, and off like a thief in the night with her best friend to save him . . . wherever in time he might be.

It is this that draws Annabelle out of her chair to stare at the sea. They're out there swimming, *she thinks, looking out on the cold dark waves of the Atlantic.* And I can't keep them safe.

◆ ◆ ◆

The lonesome house glows like a beacon through the long night. Annabelle hates when the ghosts leave her alone just before daybreak, and as darkness creeps close to dawn, she watches with regret as they drift into the woods. The yard grows quiet and still. And then . . . she hears it. The rustle through the trees, as if the leaves are whispering about something they are afraid of, before falling utterly silent.

And suddenly Annabelle sees why.

A figure stands at the edge of the yard, where the grass meets the horizon of the sea. Annabelle's hands begin to shake.

The witch standing across her yard doesn't move. She is far enough away that her face is only a white oval in the dim light. Annabelle doesn't recognize her except to know *what* she is.

"Annabelle Oaks," the witch calls across the still air, "your daughter will die."

And it feels like boulders hung around her neck, to hear such a thing.

And then the witch turns and drifts down the trail at the side of the cliff, still moments before the sun can rise. Once she's gone from view, Annabelle sinks to the floor, all the strength leaving her.

She would swim to Rosie if she could.

But no boat, no submarine, could carry her there.

There's only one way to travel through the Sea of Always. And Rosie took that with her.

CHAPTER 1

The problem with living inside the belly of a magical whale for eighty-eight days is the boredom. My best friend, Germ, and I are making the best of it by playing War.

"You got all the aces," Germ says. She is lounging on a La-Z-Boy, eating Doritos. "You always get aces."

"You're exaggerating," I say. But she's right, I do get all the aces.

I look at my hand, the wrinkled cards we've played a thousand times since boarding. My pile is huge and Germ's is dwindling. This happens all the time, and yet . . . and yet . . . somehow, even though it's purely a game of chance, Germ always wins. I'm so close to victory, I can taste it, but I'm pretty sure it will slip away.

I know this is not typically what anyone would expect to find in here, two twelve-year-old girls playing cards and stuffing their faces. To look around, you wouldn't even know we're inside an ageless, time-traveling creature at all. If anything, it looks like Germ's grammie's house, which I visited once when we were little.

Off to the right is our bedroom, with an orange rug and two beds where we sleep. Here in the center there's a TV and two beat-up La-Z-Boys, with bowls full of our favorite snacks on a table in between. There's also a dining table and a shag rug, and a treadmill and mini trampoline for Germ, who can never sit still for long.

Still, there are *some* indicators that we're not in Kansas anymore. For one thing, there's a giant glass "moonroof" above that affords us a view of the blue ocean water above. There are travel brochures littering the room that offer guidance on trips to the Stone Age, the Bronze Age, specific eras like the Han dynasty, the Gupta empire, and so on. There's also a full-color coffee-table book called *Welcome to the Sea of Always* that includes a primer on the magical creatures of the ocean of time, and a terrifying who's who profile on someone called the pirate king and his army of bones. Plus a rundown on the rules of time travel, which includes things like:

No crossing paths with your former or future self unless you want to create a troublesome wormhole.

People of the past can't see you unless they have the sight.

No returning to your starting place until your journey is at an end.

The book and brochures came in a gift basket that was waiting for us when we boarded—the kind you get from nice hotels, full of colorful tissue paper and apples and pears and a pineapple and some chocolate bars, plus spare toothpaste and some welcome papers. Germ and I long ago devoured the chocolate, tossed the fruit, and made tiny spitballs out of the tissue paper to shoot through straws at each other.

Anyway, we basically have everything two twelve-year-old girls could need while traveling through time—except our moms, and school, and humans besides each other.

Germ's theory is that the whale (whom she's named Chompy . . . since her favorite name, *Chauncey*, didn't fit right) provides everything you need for whatever kind of passenger you are, hence the Doritos and the Pop-Tarts. (The first three days, I ate Pop-Tarts until I barfed.) It also explains why there are photos of her boyfriend, D'quan Daniels, and Olympic women athletes magically pasted on the wall beside her bed, while on my side there are favorite books of mine like *The Secret Garden* and *One Crazy Summer* and *Because of Winn-Dixie*, and some of my favorites from when I was little, like *The Snowy Day*. It explains why Germ's favorite show, *LA Pet Psychic*, is on permanent loop on the TV and why we have several copies of *Pet Psychic* magazine on the coffee table. There are also cinnamon-scented candles (Germ loves cinnamon-scented candles) and matchbooks everywhere to light them.

We have everything we need. But the truth is, time feels endless inside the whale, and I guess that's because it is. I think it's safe to say that in the outside world (the one we left behind), time is passing . . . but within our whale, time stands still. I know this because I have a tiny hourglass necklace given to me by a witch, and not a grain of sand has dropped through it . . . and yet, according to Germ's watch, eighty-eight days have passed. We keep track of *that time* (home time) by marking the wall with a Sharpie (thanks, Chompy!) every time Germ's watch circles noon. So somehow time is moving, and also it's not.

Either way, we're excruciatingly bored—and so we've passed the days by trying at least fifty ways to wear eyeliner, played at least a thousand games of War, painted our toenails every color of the rainbow, had hour-long burping contests, ranked all the boys at our school back home in terms of cuteness. (Germ is devoted to D'quan but says you can't blame a girl for looking. And anyway, D'quan doesn't know the real reason why we disappeared and might think we're dead.)

We've discussed what seventh grade is going to be like if we live to see some of it, and I have promised to let Germ drag me to more parties, and promised to at least try to like her other bestie, Bibi West (who now prefers to be called by her full name, Bibiana, though we can't get used to it and always forget). We've read all the travel guides Chompy has provided. We've read and reread our most important book of all, *The Witch Hunter's Guide to the Universe*, backward and forward a thousand times. Germ has made me a special friendship bracelet to hold my whale whistle to my wrist. And now . . . we're back to War.

"Aw! Isn't Chompy sweet?" Germ squeals, looking over at a small bowl of M&M's that has appeared beside me. Staring at my M&M's, I bite my tongue. Chompy *does* seem to anticipate all our needs. (He's very subtle about it. You look away for a moment, or blink your eyes, or start to daydream, and that's when he changes things on you.) BUT Chompy also used to serve a witch (granted, the witch is dead) whose whistle now belongs to us.

"He'd probably be just as eager to provide witches whatever *they* needed," I say. "Like, we get M&M's. . . . They get cauldrons for cooking children in."

"Shh. You'll hurt his feelings," Germ hisses, glancing at the domed ceiling above us.

Chompy gives a shudder. Which makes me, for a moment, panicked. I'm always nervous that at any moment something on Chompy could go haywire. In the grand scheme of things, we're a very tiny vessel surrounded by seawater that could drown us, after all.

"See?" Germ says with accusing eyes.

"He was avoiding that octopus," I say, pointing out the moonroof at an enormous red creature floating above and past us.

Germ softens again, and she grins. "Every time I think of octopuses, I think about that time in first grade."

I lay my ace down and swipe Germ's jack, flustered. *Here we go.*

It's one of the infamous moments of my childhood. At school we were playing the Farmer in the Dell, where everyone picks partners until someone is a supposedly lonely, solitary piece of cheese. (Don't ask me, I didn't invent the special brand of torture that is the Farmer in the Dell.)

Someone had already picked Germ, so I knew I would be the cheese at the end, which would be horribly embarrassing. And so when the game was whittled down to about three people, I pointed out the window and yelled that purple eight-armed aliens were invading from outer space and we all needed to run for our lives. Somehow, I was so convincing that I got everyone to look out the window at the sky.

"That was the best," Germ says, ignoring the fact that being the girl who pretended we were being attacked by aliens turned out to be way more embarrassing than being the cheese. She lays down an ace, her only one, and we go to war. She wins with a seven to my five, and gains a bunch of cards. The next round is a war too; Germ wins again. My pile dwindles.

I feel a reluctant smile creep onto my face. Germ seems to think that all sorts of things about me are charming, things I wish I could change—like how I scowl at people I don't know and spend most of our schooltime looking out the window imagining how nice it would be to walk through a door into the clouds, away from everyone but my best friend.

She lays down a nine that brings us to war. While I've been ruminating on my shortcomings, she's managed to get the last two of my aces. Ugh.

The rest of the game follows suit. Germ's hands move quickly as she confiscates my best cards. Soon they're all gone. She looks at me apologetically.

"Sorry, Rosie, I really wanted you to win."

"That's okay," I say. "I wanted you to win too."

She yawns. "I'm gonna turn in."

Germ goes to our room and shimmies into a hot-pink pajama ensemble, provided by Chompy of course, that sets off her pale pinkish freckled cheeks and strawberry-blond hair and fits her ample frame perfectly. I change into an oversize T-shirt and sloppy flannel pants. Germ brushes her teeth and washes her face with this new cream she's been using. I run a brush over my teeth but skip the washing. Germ says "I look gorgeous" to the mirror and crawls into bed—a waterbed she's always dreamt of having. I glance at my own reflection—unbrushed brown hair, teeth too big for my mouth, shoulders too high for my neck. I've been waiting for a growth spurt all my life, and now that I'm having one, it seems like all my body parts are growing at different rates.

Germ kneels by her bed and does her nightly ritual: a Hail Mary and an Our Father. Then a prayer to the Moon Goddess for good measure. It's not all that conventional for a Catholic to believe in a goddess who lives on the moon, but Germ is her own person.

"Moon Goddess," she says to the ceiling, "please look after Ebb, wherever he is . . . even if he's nothing."

I wince; an ache flares in my chest. The last time we saw our ghost friend Ebb was the night the Time Witch came and did something terrible to him. (We'll probably never know what.) He was already dead when I knew him, but he's probably *worse* than dead now.

"And please," Germ adds, "send someone, preferably an adult, to help us kill the witches." She pops an eye open to glance at me for a second, then closes it again. "Rosie's great and all, and I'm sure she'll nail it," she says unconvincingly, "but come on, some help would be nice. Thank you."

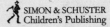

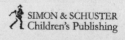